TEETH
and
SPIES

Also by Giorgio Pressburger

The Law of White Spaces

TEETH
and
SPIES

Giorgio Pressburger

Translated from the Italian by
Shaun Whiteside

Granta Books
London

Granta Publications, 2/3 Hanover Yard, London N1 8BE

First published in Great Britain by Granta Books 1999
First published in Italy as *Denti e Spie* by Rizzoli, 1994

A CIP catalogue record for this book is available from
the British Library.

1 3 5 7 9 10 8 6 4 2

ISBN 1 86207 269 8

Typeset by M Rules

Printed and bound in Great Britain by
Mackays of Chatham plc

CONTENTS

INTRODUCTION

The last time I met S.G. was in the spring of the year just past, at a convention of the Society of Psychoanalysis devoted to patients who had, for one reason or another, changed languages in the course of their life. The little seaside resort in northern Italy was deserted, the spring sun bathed the conference halls in golden light. My old acquaintance had changed a great deal since I had last seen him. His formerly thick black hair had thinned, his nose had developed even more of a curve, his eyes no longer smiled as they once had, with bitter disenchantment; his lips had grown soft, his cheeks sunk into the cavity of his mouth. 'You here too?' he asked with surprise the moment he saw me.

I should have been the one to be surprised, given that throughout his life S.G. had turned his attention to many things, but never to psychoanalysis. As for myself, I was perfectly at home here: in fact it was my plan to publish the minutes of the conference, with which I was very closely involved. Unexpectedly, however, some weeks later S.G. gave me the rights to publish a book which he described to me as the work of a friend; as far as I could tell, though, he had written it himself. 'The author,' said S.G., 'lived a very adventurous life, but did not know how to assemble all the pieces of the mosaic. The tiny tiles seemed to be scattered in space and time and he was unable to put them in order. He tried to find a way of representing the disorder, the coincidences, genuine and otherwise, the intricate interweaving of events, the pain of a life. In the end it seemed to him that he had found a solution.'

S.G. had talked to me about this book with an ingratiating insistence. Over the three days of the conference I had given him a wide berth, to avoid finding myself once again on the receiving end of his persistence. Once my work was completed I didn't even say goodbye, I just caught my flight and returned home. But when I arrived home that afternoon the concierge's office gave me an envelope. Inside was the tormented typescript of this book, sent to me by S.G. the very morning of our meeting. A note was attached to the grey folder: 'Pay attention to the dates of the events. Add them up and divide them by one hundred. It may be that the number tells you something important.'

I didn't know whether to take these instructions as an allusion to certain ancient texts or to a secret code drawn from the world of espionage, but I wasn't overly concerned. Then I read the first page, and some weeks later I acquired the publishing rights, thus becoming the editor, not of a book of psychoanalysis, but of a novel of dentistry. I printed a thousand copies, as much as my modest financial possibilities allowed; eight hundred came back.

I am glad that such a major publishing house has now decided to republish this curious little volume.

G.N.

FOREWORD

In presenting the annotations relating to the history of each of the teeth of the central character in this narrative, the editor has followed, where he has been able to, a certain chronological order, so that the reader may perhaps follow the path of the protagonist's life more clearly. Moreover, in the notebooks sent to the publishing house, the various stories were collated in a completely different way, following the order of the dental arches, beginning with the last upper right molar. There are various other ways of reading this book: for example, starting at a random page or proceeding by groups of teeth (the incisors, the canines, the premolars and the molars), and so on. The direction of the narrative will change with each method of reading, but it may be helpful to bear in mind that this novel works more or less after the fashion of today's computers; through each individual tooth the life of S.G. is examined as a whole.

For the reader wishing to follow the trail of the dental

arches, we hereby present the international notation of the permanent teeth, and below, the one invented by the author.

18	17	16	15	14	13	12	11		21	22	23	24	25	26	27	28
48	47	46	45	44	43	42	41		31	32	33	34	35	36	37	38

The graphic representation of the teeth may also be represented by the sign + for the upper teeth and by the sign − for the lower teeth. According to whether one moves to the right or to the left of the number, these signs will indicate respectively the teeth on the left and on the right. For example, +8 represents the last upper left molar, 8− the last lower right molar.

And here is the notation invented by the author. 'U' stands for upper, 'L' for lower; the second letter ('R' or 'L') indicates 'right' or 'left'.

UR8	UR7	UR6	UR5	UR4	UR3	UR2	UR1		UL1	UL2	UL3	UL4	UL5	UL6	UL7	UL8
LR8	LR7	LR6	LR5	LR4	LR3	LR2	LR1		LL1	LL2	LL3	LL4	LL5	LL6	LL7	LL8

The dates of the historical events connected to each tooth have sometimes been included, sometimes omitted, to avoid referring to things that have occurred too recently, and the attendant legal responsibilities of the case. In any case, if the author's wish was to communicate coded information through the book, he has, I feel, accomplished this.

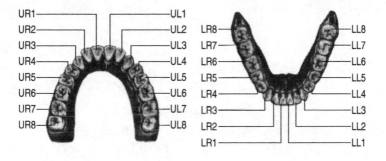

AUTHOR'S PREFACE

One day in January a tall, thin man with long white hair came into the courtyard of our building. He was wrapped in a dark green coat, torn in several places. Raising his face towards us, as we stood staring at him, he spread his arms and began to speak in a resounding voice. I was frightened, and thought that for some reason he wanted to reproach me or to curse me. My mother explained that the man was a beggar and that he was reciting something.

'Reciting? What does that mean?'

Patiently, my mother explained the meaning of the word and I listened attentively.

The beggar spoke of the various stages a man goes through, from his birth and his time of wailing in the cradle, to the time when he becomes a man, combative and quick to anger, and finally to the time when he once more becomes weak and feeble, his strength drained away. 'Last scene of all, that ends this strange eventful history, is second childishness

and mere oblivion, sans teeth, sans eyes, sans taste, sans everything.'

As he spoke of extreme old age, he took out his false teeth,
drawled the words and hissed the sibilants to accentuate the
signs of his own infirmity. When he uttered the words 'sans
everything', he dropped his arms and began to sob distress-
ingly: now he was no longer 'reciting', he was living, and
enacting his own terrible misery. We threw him a small coin,
as did some of the other people who lived in our building.
The beggar – an old out-of-work actor – remained where he
was, drying his tears, and then, after standing motionless for a
few seconds, he silently picked up the coins that had fallen on
the yellow tiles of the courtyard and, without a word of
thanks, his eyes fixed on the ground, he went away. My
mother, genuinely moved, whispered 'poor thing', and went
back to cook the dinner.

The image of that man with his suddenly hollow cheeks,
who managed to age thirty years from one moment to the
next (and whose dentures conferred upon him the appearance
of one who was not yet decrepit) has always stayed with me.
When I think of him I feel like a child again, one who has still
to pass through all the stages of life, rather than the old man
that I really am. I must confess that my mind has played this
trick on me at least thirty-two times, the number, that is, of
my teeth. In fact, the day the old actor appeared in our courtyard was the beginning of the constant attention I paid to my
teeth, my obsession with them.

From that day, my tongue began to explore my teeth each
morning after I woke up and to supply my brain with information on the tiniest scratch, the tiniest movement, the tiniest

novelty. Although it was not because of this that I became an assiduous visitor to dentists, of whom, like everyone else, I have always been rather frightened. But dentists have also become my best friends, the witnesses to my life. The story of each tooth is a particular story, worth the telling. Each tooth in a sense encapsulates our entire character, that which is called the 'ego'. Or maybe we tend to attribute a particular function to each of them. Teeth are, for those of us who keep them till we die, our final message across the centuries to posterity: our smile, our grimace of rage or envy to the person rummaging in the dust, perhaps thousands of years hence, who finds the remains of our fleeting presence on the earth. But even if we lose them, in dental surgeries, in battles or in bar-room brawls, they remain as testimony to what our lives have been from the moment we enter the world: a continuous state of deprivation.

It is not my wish to depress the reader. The pleasures that the teeth and gums can give us are among the most refined. I shall attempt to discuss those too, since if I have decided to write these stories it is only because I find something extraordinary in them.

It would be interesting to do the same thing with each individual cell of our bodies. Perhaps in some not-too-distant future there will be a machine capable of recording and describing, cell by cell, moment by moment, all the experiences of a human body, from birth to death. But how many generations would it take to read that vast book from start to finish? And more importantly, will the universe last long enough to do so?

MILK OR 'DECIDUOUS' TEETH

In the course of his life, man goes through two sets of teeth. The first, inexplicable eruption of something alien in one of the most sensitive parts of our body, our gums, begins after a few months of life and is the source of terrible pain. 'What is this agony?' our consciousness wonders, seized by uncontrollable panic. Our whole being is in turmoil, because we don't yet know what a question or an answer is. All we know is the anguish of something hurting us from within. How can we make the pain stop? Time and again our tongue runs over that smooth, moist point in our mouth where all that exists is eternal pain, without cause, without origin.

The eruption of the first tooth sums up the world for us.

Something hard is blossoming within our body's tissue, in order to hurt us. We are hurting ourselves, we are alien to ourselves, our own enemies. All our lives will be nothing but a repetition of pain. If the breast and its warm milk were the source of pleasure, now, in our mouth where once that beneficial liquid flowed, there is only pain. That is the first tooth. That pain is repeated a number of times as the other teeth erupt – only twenty of these deciduous ones – until we learn that this something that has grown within us, causing us pain, can also be a source of pleasure. One day we discover how we can use our teeth to crush and dismember something soft (or even something slightly harder): food. And this hard thing can also destroy that which is disagreeable to us.

At the age of one – my memory has trouble going back so far – I bit my mother, in the skin between her index finger and her thumb, while she was trying to put a spoonful of medicine into my mouth. The War was raging then; illnesses and infections fell upon houses like splinters of bombs or grenades. 'The War' I have written, as if since the dawn of the existence of *Homo sapiens* there had been only 'that' war, the most important event in the world. For a long time 'the War', as I saw it, the gigantic and violent World War that hurled pus-green corpses into the virgin snow of our district, seemed the beginning of the world. Now I know that's not how it was. The most important event must surely have been the eruption of the first milk tooth in the mouth of the first *Homo sapiens*.

In a hesitant voice, and unable to restrain herself, she screamed. 'That scream was the *Urschrei*, the primordial scream from which music originated,' my great friend Maestro

G. said to me one day. He didn't find me in complete agreement, since the scream was, in my view, rather the beginning
of speech. It actually made a big impression on me to feel how
my hard tooth could make me scream with pain, and not
only me but my mother as well. Her pain was alien to me,
unimaginable, and yet there it was, my mother was screaming
as I had screamed when that piece of me was emerging from
my flesh. Someone else, someone outside of me, was screaming. It was my first dialogue in sounds. It spoke of pain. The
pain of the erupting tooth and the pain the tooth causes when
it bites, and the pain of giving birth and of being born: the
pain of being alive.

But those milk teeth were really my first instruments of
pleasure. Even when I wasn't hungry, driven onwards by an
inexorable inner goad, I felt the impulse to gnaw everything.
I felt that terrible impulse for several years. Then those little
teeth began to move in their sockets. As I sat in the kitchen in
our house on Hire Car Street, absorbed in my first school
homework, I would push them back and forth with my
tongue. It was very pleasurable to feel them moving, those
teeth which for the previous few years had seemed so immobile, so powerful, so hard. To my tongue, this feeling was also
the instrument of my enjoyment. Forty years later, Maestro G.
would give me very helpful explanations about this phenomenon. But more of that later. If the tip of my tongue pushed
UL6, moving immediately afterwards to LR6, I felt dizzy as
though I had been flying over enormous distances, and I was
filled with an unimaginable sensation of sweetness.

Not even my mother's caresses ever gave me such a strange
feeling of well-being, such a subtle form of tension so close to

pleasure. My imagination magnifies those little white pearls born from my flesh: as I sent them rocking back and forth, I saw them, in my mind's eye, as big as the foot of the kitchen table, as big as the cupboard. Our imagination can change the dimensions of the world, it can make reality disproportionate. But knowledge is based precisely on this lack of proportion. Should we perhaps, as so much Oriental philosophy suggests, distract our minds from things, and focus on the void, where no comparisons exist? During those first few years of life my oral cavity became the universe where pain and pleasure mingled unpredictably. That combination is absurd, I now know, it is the goad that forces us, like oxen, to continue our journey right to the end, right to the slaughter. The ramifications of the fifth cranial nerve which, leaving the brain, descend into the eyes, the nose and the maxilla, are to a great extent the source of many of our ills. The teeth, which we consider symbolically as manifestations of our aggressiveness, are also the measure of the good and evil that the world has in store for us.

In that dark kitchen, the child playing with his milk teeth in the long winter afternoons, waiting for his mother to return, was, unwittingly, coming to terms with good and evil.

Then came the moment of detachment. Those painful excrescences of the self began to part from the flesh. One day, a tooth fell into my soup, leaving in its place a pulsing, bleeding gap. One of the keys to my pleasure and my pain had ended up outside of my body. Thus, with dismay, I noticed that the other keys were, in their disorderly fashion, preparing to leave too. But the outlines of the new and 'permanent' teeth were waiting in the wings. There they were, preparing to torment me: even to imagine them hurt my flesh. The new pain lasted for years, decades, until the eruption of my final wisdom tooth. But this is the beginning of another adventure in the universe of the oral cavity, no different, perhaps, from the cave in which, according to Plato, our soul resides.

FROM MY FATHER'S DIARY

Recently, looking through old family papers, I found my father's prison diary. From it I quote some pages concerning myself. It is a lined notebook, bound in black woven paper. The text is written in pencil. Certain words are faded, illegible.

20 April 1944
Tomorrow they will take me far from my family. We will be transferred to Transylvania in a punishment unit to work in a stone quarry. Today one of my son's little teeth fell out. Rather than 'giving it to the Tooth Fairy', I put it in a little leather bag and sewed it into my overcoat. I hope it will help

me to return home. I don't understand at all. Just because I was born into a certain family, a certain people, they are deporting me. Who allowed this to happen?

30 September 1944
War, war.
Sarah sent me another little tooth. Attached to its neck was a little blood. Might it be a sign? But maybe not everything is a sign of something. Maybe not everything exists.

3 December 1944
Escaped from the camp. I clenched my son's little tooth between my own. I hope it saves me.

4 December 1944
I've swallowed my son's tooth.

5 December 1944
I didn't see my son's tooth leave my body with my dung. I am hiding in a school that has been turned into a hospital. I am cutting off the hands and feet of wounded men, my trade as a ritual butcher is a great help.

4 January 1945
They are going to shoot us. Who will defend me? Everything is disappearing, but everything leaves its mark . . . in the void.

1 February 1945
There's fighting in the streets. Two toes on my right foot frozen. Japan still at war, and Manchuria. But not even these

names mean anything to me. Faces disappear, words, thoughts, worlds disappear. Found my son's tooth in my right boot. Its imprint on my frozen big toe.

13 February 1945
The army of 'liberation' has come. The enemies were about to destroy the whole district, to kill us *en masse*. Who knows why they didn't? I dreamed I was slaughtering again, at the local slaughterhouse. The cows I had killed had begun to denounce me. I opened my mouth to answer that I wasn't responsible for the invention of life and death. But I had no teeth, I couldn't speak.

August 1945
I'm home. The first adult tooth has appeared in my son's mouth. In Japan a city disappeared in three minutes. Which event is more important? The appearance of the tooth, or the disappearance of the city? I'm not going to write any more in this notebook. I shall go back to slaughtering.

20 September 1945
I slaughtered a kid for the gentry . . . I don't have lice in my hair now. I wonder if there's any sense in going on living without lice, without hunger, without terror.

UL6

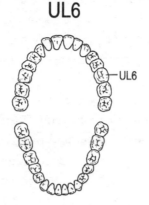

UL6

A few words on the secondary dentition. At the age of about six I realized the importance of the phenomenon that is the growth of the permanent teeth. My mother explained to me, with the patience and gentleness that made her so indispensable to my upbringing, that the new pain, the new sore points in my gums were the harbinger of something that I would have to keep safe and take with me to the end of my days. I was dismayed none the less, and started weeping.

'To the end of my days? Am I going to die soon?' I asked her.

She stroked my head. 'The Eternal One has preserved us from war. All our relations died in that bloodbath, but He granted our family a little grace. For you, I pray that you keep your new teeth for a hundred and twenty years, and for me, I pray that I will never see you dead. There is no greater pain for a mother than to see her own children die. I pray you will bury me, and that afterwards you will live in peace for years, amen.'

During this time my father came home from prison, and while I stood at the mirror looking inside my mouth to study the cruciform clefts in which the white of the enamel was already showing through, he encouraged me, saying, 'That's what life's like, each day a piece of us dies and another is born. Our bodies copy the ebb and flow of life and death on earth.'

My mother showed me how to brush my teeth with toothbrush and toothpaste, my father explained the difference between incisors, canines, premolars and molars, briefly outlining the function of each. And so my consciousness accepted as part of my person those gleaming, cutting entities, so alien to the rest of my body that they seemed in a sense to come from outside of me. According to my mother, I was to look after them because, once they were lost, they could be replaced only by fake ones.

Every day I stood in front of the mirror spying on the changes that were taking place in the red flesh of my mouth. My last remaining milk tooth, the upper left first incisor, was extracted from me with some difficulty. In a sense, while the army of the other teeth had already grown in my mouth to warn me of the battle that I should soon have to fight 'tooth and nail', so to speak, part of me was refusing to leave childhood behind. That small, unstable sign of the final years of childhood remained attached to my maxilla. One winter afternoon my father tied it to a piece of white thread and said to me: 'Close your eyes and don't move.' I obeyed. I heard him fiddling about and at a certain point I felt him grab me by the shoulders and yank me hard. A terrible pain shot through my face. Immediately afterwards, my mother pressed my head to her breast and held me there, whispering gentle words and stroking my back. When I pulled away, in floods of tears, her shirt was stained with blood. Tied with the thread to the window-catch, my last milk tooth dangled like a hanged man. My father gave me a shot of rum to rinse my mouth, and then went to bed.

That pain signalled the end of my unhappy childhood. Now I felt I was a member of a stronger community, the community of adults. Years of peace and well-being followed; I went to elementary school and primary school (as the first eight classes were called in those days), convinced now that the agony that returned to my mouth from time to time was the pain that would forge the future fighter for the trials of life, and that those hard, gleaming weapons, born from within my 'self', were there for all time, not for death. I was certain that I would keep them for ever, brushing them carefully and taking great care of them. One day, our teacher took us to a dental clinic. My faith in the goodness of creation began to crack. This is why.

After a visit lasting a few minutes, the young dentist who had made me sit down in an iron chair, its back upholstered in leather, called me back a few days later for a further session. I was to go on my own, not with the rest of the class. The treatment I needed would, obviously, be free of charge. 'What

treatment?' I asked fearfully. I felt completely healthy and
invulnerable. 'Two or three small problems, nothing to worry
about. You've got good teeth, but the war and the lack of calcium have left their mark on you. Don't be frightened. You'll
see, the lady dentist who is going to treat you is an angel.'

I reported the outcome of this visit to my parents. They
immediately looked in my mouth, touching my teeth, and
each exclaimed in turn: 'Oh, look at that little black spot! And
there's another one!'

I smelt the strange odour of their fingers: it was the first
time that strange hands had penetrated my body. Once I was
on my own, I took my mother's little mirror and looked in
my mouth as well. There were little black spots on three of
my teeth. 'I thought I was stainless, intact, impregnable, and
now the colour of night is invading my body. Why are you
doing this to me?' I exclaimed. But I recovered from that
doubt, from that terror, the following week, in the dental
surgery. The dentist who greeted me was the most beautiful
creature I had ever seen. The white complexion of her face
was adorned with two pink flowers around her cheekbones,
her perfectly outlined, full lips were the very image of discretion and kindness, her big blue eyes seemed filled with
astonishment and friendly concern. Her blonde hair, soft and
misty, was gathered together at the nape of her neck and
looked like golden filigree. The minute I saw her I wished my
teeth, all twenty-eight of them, to be diseased, seriously diseased, so that the treatment could go on for years.

When the dentist invited me, almost in a whisper, to make
myself comfortable in the iron chair, I felt a sense of shame,
the memory of which terrifies me even today. Not having

brushed my teeth, I smelt my breath on that first winter afternoon: it was heavy, imbued with the odours of food
masticated by the salivary juices. As she plucked fragments of
meat from the gaps with the probe, I just wanted to sink into
the ground. 'I'm an ugly, imperfect, impure creature!' I
thought. 'Man is horrible. He is putrid, corrupt!' I went on
repeating to myself. And she, the angel, was lovingly taking
care of me, washing my sullied flesh with jets of water from a
rubber bulb. When the drill, activated by her little feet,
entered my decaying teeth, I thought not of the searing pain,
but of my shame. She introduced a filling made of pieces of
cotton wool, ether and I don't know what else, in each of the
three open holes in the enamel and the dentine, and then
made an appointment for four days later. The three teeth
affected by the pain were UL6, LR4 and UR5. But here I
only wish to speak of UL6, because that was the molar that
gave me my first sense of the quality of pain and the meaning
of existence.

The day of the second session, I didn't eat when I got back
from school. In love as I was with the dentist, nothing in the
world would have made me repel her again with the waste
matter in my mouth. The afternoon was particularly gloomy.
A dirty slush covered the streets. Once homework was over,
an hour and a half before the appointment, I started to clean
my teeth, running the brush over them time and again, turning the toothpaste to white foam. Sitting by the ceramic basin
I thought of the dentist, evoking her angelic image in my
mind. In my thoughts, my very breath was becoming revolting. So it was that I discovered the vaguely unpleasant smell of
my breath, still bitter from lunch.

I had paid little attention to my body's odours: in the toilet I had noticed the smell of my parents' excreta, particularly that of my mother. One day, my father had terrified me with the story of a man who, five minutes before his wedding, went to the bathroom and, hearing a sound coming from the adjacent toilet, suspected that it was caused by the gases from the bowels of his bride. When, leaning against the door, he convinced himself that his suspicions were well founded, he made off without a word, abandoning the wedding. After hearing that story, I was horrified at the idea that my bowels might produce such noisy and malodorous fumes. But until the age of sixteen, apart from two or three cases of diarrhoea, I noticed nothing of the kind in myself. Now, as I faced another session with the beautiful dentist, I was terrified by the possibility that I might repel her. I ran to the bathroom, picked up a little bottle of eau de cologne and poured it into my mouth. The yellowish liquid tasted revolting, and burned my oral membrane terribly, but at least I was sure of making a good impression on the woman I loved. I wanted to seem different from the way I was, I was ashamed of everything, of the rumbling of my stomach, of the colour of my hair. I was ashamed to belong to the human race.

That day, the dentist filled UL6 and arranged a third appointment for me. In her face I found the same signs of mute benevolence that I had discerned in her the time before. UL6 retained that filling for fifty years. It was the third to last tooth to leave me, and there is a truly macabre significance in that fact since, on my third appointment, the dentist confided something really appalling. First of all she asked if the tooth she had just filled had given me any pain during the week.

When I replied that it hadn't, she said smoothly: 'And it couldn't have. I've killed it. I've killed the nerve with arsenic. That tooth, sadly, is dead, but you will be able to use it until it falls out.' So, death had entered me and I hadn't even noticed. UL6, in fact, murdered before it could trouble me thanks to the dentist's foresight, never gave me any pain. Something had issued from my self, something represented by that foreign body within me, that hard, white 'other'. It was death. Because I could still chew with UL6, and because I had it within me for so long, I was able to forget that part of me was already a corpse. But there was something worse than that, as I was to discover some years later.

UR5

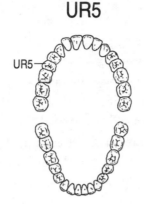

UR5

For me, the story of UR5 has parallels with that of Revelation. Until the age of eighteen I would never have thought that a tooth could be the link between myself and the great mystery. When my mother, peremptory and insistent, taught me the movements I had to carry out to brush my teeth, I didn't doubt in the slightest that her instructions were sound. Unfortunately, as I was to discover a number of years later, they were wrong in every detail. With that horizontal movement of the brush I was destroying the outermost stratum of the dental structure, the enamel, and also contributing to the erosion of the gums and their bony setting. But the excessive consumption of sugar and honey was probably the cause of my first caries. During the war years I had been hungry and had experienced prolonged periods of childhood anxiety, for which, in adulthood, sweets had become my consolation. Feeding on these, bacteria found the perfect terrain to proliferate in my mouth.

But as we now know, the spread of colonies of bacteria in our oral cavity is the chief cause of the destruction of the wonderful architecture of the dental arch. In my case, the first, horrible abyss opened up at around the age of thirteen, as I was approaching manhood. But the decay spread silently and unobserved. The revelation of its destruction didn't occur for a further five years. During that time, a bloody revolution broke out in my country, and I too wanted to see myself in the front line, a protagonist of that important moment in history.

When I heard the first shots and saw the first fires flickering, I ran on to the balcony where the cold October air whipped my face. While I was watching the flames rising from the offices of the newspaper *Freedom of the People*, I became aware of a searing pain in my mouth, in the area around the second upper right premolar, UR5. My mind was filled with a sense of freedom; in the distant, obscure singing I recognized the signs of the birth of something that would change many people's lives. After decades of obtuse restrictions, freedom was returning. Freedom! The expansion of consciousness through space and time, the unrestricted and eternal play of the human spirit in pursuit of self-definition! I watched those flames, resolving deep within myself to join the stream of happy people that was growing in the streets of my city. I too started to shout, from that balcony, towards the deafening clatter of rifle fire. But the moment I opened my mouth, a terrible twinge ran through my maxilla. I had never known exactly what the maxilla was, or that I had such a sensitive bone in my body.

The twinge (what an inadequate word that is . . .) lasted an instant and then vanished. I ran home and put on my coat, ready to go out. My mother, not knowing how to hold me back – I was utterly insensitive to her concern – begged me at least to take a little tea or a few spoonfuls of soup: who knew what time I would get back, and in the meantime I would get hungry. To avoid feeding her anxiety, I agreed. I followed her into the kitchen and swallowed down the hot soup. In fact I didn't get beyond the first few spoonfuls because that accursed premolar began to give an even more terrible twinge. When my father heard what was going on, he declared, with his usual optimism, that the pain would soon disappear in the face of the only thing that really interested me at that time: being a witness to history. Then he gave me a little bottle of rum. 'Take it with you, and if you feel any pain, take a sip and keep it between your tongue and your cheek, close to the tooth that's hurting. It'll pass, you'll see. And now off you go and be careful.'

I ran down the stairs three at a time, in a flash I was at the gate, just as old Roth was about to close it.

'Don't go out,' he growled, 'there are so many bullets flying through the air, why seek out danger if you don't have to?'

'Moments like this only come along once in your life,' I answered. 'Let me out, I beg you, Uncle Roth.'

The old man took the big black key from his coat pocket and opened up. Once I was in the street I started running for the junction of the Great Joseph Ring and the People's Theatre. Hardly had I run twenty yards before I had the third terrible, unmistakable stab of pain.

I stopped, but the pain was still searing: I had never felt anything like it. I tried to go on, opening my mouth to let the fresh air in, but there was nothing to be done: while I was running towards freedom, running away from myself, that pain called me back to my ineptitude and pettiness, to my loneliness. And it worsened. I clung on, fastened on to my pain, because now it was rising up, rising along that nerve path, a few inches long, the trigeminus, across my face to my brain and then out of my skull, out of me and upwards. Tied to that invisible thread, I was suspended in the void, alone with my suffering. Then, in a flash, a thought came to me: someone is holding the other end of the thread, someone is holding me tied to myself and to him, this pain is keeping us tied to one another. With my weeping eyes turned skywards – the pain had probably spread to the lachrymal gland – I heard my own voice shouting inside me: 'What do you want? What do you want?' Then, in an angry movement, I took out the little bottle of rum, took a few sips, with the muscles of my tongue and my cheek I pressed the liquid against the decayed tooth and, head down, walked towards the flames. The remedy my father had suggested remained effective for a quarter of an hour. In the meantime, I rejoined the crowd, mingled with the shouting people, uniting my voice with theirs, my fist held aloft along with all the others.

'Multitudes, I embrace you!' I chanted, while I was dragged along in the slow, irregular flow of the crowd. When we approached Parliament, the effect of the rum wore off and I vomited with pain. I felt as if my head wanted to detach itself from my body, to follow the line of that suffering, but I was also aware of the dogged grey persistence of the pain. Making an effort of which I would never again be capable as long as I lived, I broke away from the flood of people and huddled in a doorway, weeping and repeating: 'What do you want from me? Set me free!' I beat my head against the broken, dusty cobbled wall. I drained the contents of the bottle and, drunk and deaf, tottered homewards repeating the obsessive thought to myself: 'These are the terrible chains. I should be grateful for that, and instead I'm suffering. These are the chains!' But this idea disappeared later that evening, when my father, heedless of the late hour, phoned Dr Lissauer and then dragged me down to his practice on Karpfenstein Street. The dentist examined the tooth with the Barzy lever and the concave mirror, and every time I cried out he repeated: 'Why are you shouting? It's hurting you, not me. What do you want from me with your shouting?'

This absurd declaration of his imperviousness to pain persuaded me to be calm. In the end, the dentist gave me an injection, prescribed some pills to take three times a day and made an appointment for a week later. 'We'll be able to save the tooth,' he announced. And in fact, with a second filling, he saved it. Ten years later, Dr Lissauer hanged himself from a window of his clinic. The constant presence of physical pain had so infected him as to rule out any future. In his suicide note he wrote only: 'It's not worth it.' It is not clear whether this referred to life or the death by suicide that was in some way prefigured the moment he jotted down those words.

I took that filling with me on my travels abroad. On the

occasion of the fifth mission assigned to me by the State
Export Company, I had to travel to the Middle East. I was
crossing the Sinai desert, which was overrun with armoured
cars, and I cannot rule out the idea that the little amalgam filling fell out there without my noticing. Dr Lissauer's gesture as
he mixed the amalgam in his mortar, pounding the substance
with the pestle, was as real to me as the hand that put the seal
on my pain in the desert was mysterious. Hardly had I left
those places behind when UR5 began to give me a great deal
of pain. I returned to my homeland tortured by unbearable
twinges which at night sent me tossing and turning like a man
demented. Neither sleeping pills nor ablutions of cognac or
rum could free me from that agony: my whole brain res-
onated with that inextinguishable presence confined in the
maxillary bone. Rachel, my wife, wept, kissed me, pressed me
to her bosom, in vain.

One evening I called my father to ask him for the address of
a dentist; I didn't know who had replaced Dr Lissauer. After
a brief consultation with my mother, he gave me the phone
number of Dr Aaron Schwartz, his companion on the 'A.
Nimzowitsch' chess team. Without the slightest compunction
I got the old dentist out of his bed and, discovering who I
was, he called me to his house. Upon seeing me he was
gripped by a strange and sudden fervour: while we were waiting for the anaesthetic injection to take effect, so as to proceed
with the extraction of the tooth, Schwartz suggested a game
of chess. After putting the Thomson forceps, the Lecleuze
lever and the McDonald tweezers boiling on a spirit burner in
a chrome container, he took an old and greasy chessboard
from a white cupboard.

'If you win, I won't make you pay for the extraction, and if I win, we'll put off the operation until tomorrow,' he said.

'No! I won't be able to wait that long!'

'Then sharpen your wits. Don't you know that pain and desperation are the very things that spur man onwards? Certainly contentment, or – to use that ridiculous word – happiness aren't the motors of life. OK, you're white.'

Dr Schwartz, out of negligence, out of avarice, or perhaps on purpose, had put too little Novocaine in his injection, so that the pulsating pain didn't actually go away, but was merely attenuated. It was in this demented condition that I resorted to the old Italian opening, even in those days considered none too favourable to the white player.

I couldn't stop moving, I contorted myself on the chair, I crouched in on myself, my own instrument of torture for anyone who wanted to put me to the test. Schwartz, like an old satyr, leaned over the chessboard, pondering each move for a long time.

This gave the pain the opportunity to revive in all its violence. The game lasted over an hour, and I really had to muster all my forces to beat him. Dr Schwartz was not a good player, but in these conditions it was all I could do to predict future moves and positions. Everything was concentrated in that intense moment of suffering. The dentist refused to surrender, preferring to endure checkmate.

'I beg you, take the tooth out now!' I yelled as I made the victorious move.

Schwartz, before proceeding to what dentists call the 'avulsion' of the tooth, was preparing himself with minute attention to every detail. 'Well done, young man, you've really earned this extraction!' said the old man, and I, my heart beating, reflected that the piece of my body that he was taking away for good, would, indeed, be seriously dead, gone for eternity.

I asked Dr Schwartz not to throw away the extracted tooth, perhaps deceiving myself that, if kept in a box, that premolar would remain alive in some way. I was disappointed in this as well, because as a result of the slow twisting movements the tooth split and Schwartz had to resort to a laborious operation to recover the roots. I almost lost my senses with pain, I was close to vomiting, I felt as though my brain was being pulled down through my root canals. I shrieked, I groaned, while the dentist rummaged in my gums with his tweezers. Feeling the salt taste of my blood in my mouth, I thought: 'This is what the death agony is like. It isn't enough to disappear, we have to earn death by suffering. Why?'

When Dr Schwartz said: 'OK, we've finished,' I was filled with a sudden and genuine happiness.

'It's over!' I mentally exclaimed. 'It's over,' as if I had just vanquished the enemy, death. The pain lasted another two or three days, during which my tongue ceaselessly followed the route which, from that bloody chasm, led upwards, outside of me, towards a point to which I was tied by the terrible thread of pain.

LR3

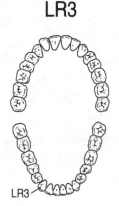

LR3

When, as a child, I first saw a piano, I immediately thought of teeth. The ivory keyboard with its black gaps called to mind the white enamel of the dental arches. Some years later, when I began to study my own body with determined objectivity, I realized that my teeth, like a musical instrument, produced a wide variety of sounds, quite apart from that familiar sound of chattering teeth as a result of fever or fear.

The most impressive sound for me came from one particular tooth, the lower right canine: LR3. Because of an erratic thrust of the roots, this tooth, when I was about twenty years old, began to sag to the left, partially masking its neighbouring incisor, which was pushed backwards towards the inside of

the oral cavity. The tip of my tongue began systematically to
strike the intruder, but there was nothing to be done: LR3
wouldn't draw back. This irregularity, this deformity, also
gave me a constant sensitivity in the gums and the nerve of
that canine, which transmitted the signal 'salty taste' to the
cerebral cortex. Hardly had the noise and the anxieties of the
day subsided before that signal sounded, emerging into my
consciousness.

One night I took my first ever train journey, to a remote
little village inhabited by Swabians, where, along with my
university companions, I was to organize a soirée dedicated to
the culture of that people. For many weeks we had been
rehearsing their poetry and songs, and suddenly German no
longer seemed to me the lofty, unparalleled language of
Goethe or Schiller or Heine, or the bestial language of the
soldiers who had been on the point of killing me on more
than one occasion during the war, but the spoken language of
peaceful peasants going about their everyday life with stubborn slowness.

The train bumped and jolted, and I was kept awake
through the night. My travelling companion, Erika, exuded
the scent of a blossoming young girl. I thought about the
future, about what life would have in store for me, but also
about how to get my hands on Erika's legs and breasts. To
divert my mind from such risky thoughts, I sought to turn my
imagination in a different direction. I made plans for the
future: I would have liked to become a military adviser in
some country or other, or an astronaut, or maybe both at the
same time.

While I was elaborating these fantasies, my tongue began to

stick to the inner face of LR3 like a suction cap. Then, all of a sudden, it broke away and the tooth made an imperceptible movement, a faint click between its two neighbours. This click produced a sound which, amplified by the cranial bone, was similar to that of a guitar string plucked by a plectrum. It was a flat sound, dull and dissonant, a faithful representation of life. From that night onwards, in moments of abandon, my tongue surrendered to the temptation of sounding that 'string'. A long dialogue began between LR3 and my brain. That hard white mass had ceased to be merely a weapon against other people, against myself, or a mere instrument devoted to mastication, but a perennial interlocutor in the silences of consciousness. Music had entered me.

It was a time when I was beginning to go to concerts of classical music, and to listen to all the subtle resonances of my body: the gurgling of my gastric juices, the beating of my heart, the sound of my lungs and, of course, the click produced by LR3. I had wanted to stupefy myself, to dodge the discomfort, to wrap myself up in a kind of fog, but the pain re-entered me, subtle and unavoidable, in the form of music. My conscience now held not only silence and everyday noise, but also music in all its forms, from German, Romanian, Slovak, Bulgarian popular songs to the *Lieder* of Schubert, the melodramas of the great Verdi, all the way down to the dull, muffled click of my tooth sucked by my tongue, to the eternal music of molecules, of suffering matter. It was during this time that I first saw Maestro G. conducting, the person who would be a presence in my life for a number of years.

At a dance given by the central committee of the youth section of the Party (in that distant past there was in my country only one political party, called the Workers' Party), I met Rachel, serene, wise, relaxed and enthusiastic about the future. After eight months we married in the courtyard of the Temple on Grand Transport Street. To avoid compromising our reputation as staunch materialists, the ceremony was held in secret.

We had our honeymoon, like many couples similar to ourselves, in a spa resort. I should say that my greatest diversion, on this occasion, was to listen at sunset, on the shores of the lake, to the click of LR3. I didn't exactly think of Rachel as a woman, more as a friend, a good substitute for my mother but without her attractiveness.

On my return home, the music within me was silenced by the illustrious orthognathic surgeon Schlesinger.

I went to him on the advice of Dr Lissauer who, during a check-up, brought to my attention the slight change that had occurred in my physiognomy over the past few years. I had never heard of orthognathic surgery, the science that deals with the chewing apparatus, the teeth, the maxilla, the mandible, and their functions, and has the task of rectifying the malpositions of those parts of the body. Through congenital defect or inadequate care, this apparatus may fall prey to what is called malocclusion, which is to say the distorted closure of the two dental arches: the maxilla may protrude forwards, the mandible retract, or vice versa. In my case, the continuous pushing by my tongue on LR3 and a probable hereditary factor had pushed the mandible forward, giving my face a slightly concave conformation. This was a Class III malocclusion, the notorious 'inverted bite' in Angle's classification. This defect might hinder my plans, I thought, and prevent me from being taken on as an aspiring astronaut, not to speak of any later military career I might have had in mind.

South East Asia had been invaded by a major world power, two antithetical notions of the world had launched a battle against one another in the forests and glades of an ancient land. Free competition in commerce and industry confronted a rigorous defence of labour; almost unlimited individual freedom stood face to face with an organization whose chief aim was to preserve the state and the idea of equality. The first of these, the invader, was powerful and had access to the most modern discoveries of military science, while the latter had at its disposal lives and a millennial wisdom, apart from the long-distance support it had from another great military power, but one which limited itself only to the supply of arms and expertise. Whatever else might have been behind the scenes of that war, I don't know to this day. After having followed those bloody events, for hours and hours, in newspapers and on television, one day it occurred to me that for the first time since man had reflected upon his own destiny, since he had developed a consciousness, at least one of two competing parties was not fighting a war in order to win it, but just in order to make war, sinking into it energy, money and human lives.

I was still disappointed at this time, but in the mean time I had been wearing, for a good 0.6 years, the Delair mask and then the Harvey appliance, in the hope of rectifying the arrangement of my teeth, my maxilla and my mandible, and so having the chance to be an astronaut or a military attaché. The Delair mask was a kind of cage that went around my head, making me a prisoner both of myself and of whoever had put it on me. Watching, breathing, speaking, even thinking always made me more aware of that state of imprisonment and the impossibility of escaping it. After seven months, the Delair mask was taken away from me one day, and I was then filled with a terrible panic as I became aware that a phase had come to an end. In the mean time my life had changed direction: I was entrusted with secret little tasks that I was unable to refuse. My physiognomy had returned to the way it was before I began to 'play' LR3.

Maestro G., before he became my mortal enemy, spoke to me one day of a famous composition dedicated to the sounds of the belly, but he made no mention of the muffled sound of a tooth. I can no longer produce that music, however, that flat sound with my canine and my tongue. I might add that LR3 was one of the last teeth to leave me. Having reached the age of sixty, I had it extracted in a dental clinic: resisting to the last, it became incompatible with the installation of a set of dentures. The moment it was extracted from me, with a faint rip, I heard the sound of that 'string'. 'Remember me,' my tooth seemed to be saying, 'remember the music, that supreme expression of the spirit which, like Socrates, every-one would be able to hear at the moment of death, if we were spiritual beings. But we are not.' Rachel, who went with me to the clinic, collected the tooth and put it in a matchbox.

We went back to our apartment on Karpfenstein Street. When Gerson, my son, had to set off for the Middle East as military adviser to an Arab country, Rachel gave him LR3 as a lucky charm. Our son returned safe and sound from that demented war: in two months he had learned to play the guitar and to suffer the anguish of a constant and invisible menace. He had understood the essence of life.

THE WISDOM TEETH

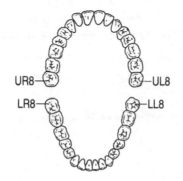

UR8—
LR8—
—UL8
—LL8

For me, the story of the four wisdom teeth is that of the four Horsemen of the Apocalypse. This is not to say that the attainment of wisdom (how many brutal crimes have been committed in the name of reason) is the equivalent of that ultimate catastrophe. My final molars emerged at a time of bloody events, and bloody events have always accompanied their existence. In the end, even their leaving was marked with blood, since they were torn violently from their sockets. But each of these four tetragons living as guests in my skull had a different character from the others, just like the four evangelists, the four humours described by Aristotle, the four Horsemen, the four kinds of judgement: moral, critical,

aesthetic and philosophical. Each of these teeth expressed its
own way of being or not being in the world. I have noticed
this all through the long course of my life: I have followed
them attentively, noting everything connected to them in my
life and in the events of my century. I have been the scribe of
those four silent authors of my history – the history of someone in possession of wisdom, and thus constantly anticipating
the worst.

UL8

The upper left eight tooth emerged when I was eighteen. I
looked at my red flesh with the help of my mother's mirror, a
little piece of rectangular glass covered on the back by a thin
layer of mercury. Yes, the mirror, that mysterious reflection of
the world, was made with the same material that was used to
fill the holes made in my teeth by the bacteria. One day, the
inflamed flesh of my gums parted and, with shrewd and silent
ostentation, UL8 emerged. It stayed there like a little virgin,
showing and hiding itself at the same time. Two days later my
father gave me a gold Doxa wristwatch, and my mother
invited twenty relatives to dinner.

'You will have to remember this party for your whole life,'
my mother said to me.

'From today you are an adult, capable of commanding your
instincts,' my father murmured. 'Try to remember.'

'How can you command your instincts?' I asked. 'They're
so fast, they're always ahead of you. You have hardly time to
formulate a thought, and they've already got their claws into
you.'

'Every time you brush your teeth you have to repeat to yourself: "I've got a wisdom tooth and I want to keep it, just as I want to keep my wisdom."'

'That's all it takes as far as you're concerned? You think you can fight off bad instincts by brushing your teeth?'

'Yes, my son, the obtuseness of the instincts can only be fought with the obtuseness of perseverance.'

I was very struck by my father's statement, and felt inspired by it. That day really was like the coming of the Messiah. Rather than wisdom, what seemed to have descended upon me was a fresh ability to understand the world. I spent months and months with this radiant feeling, I felt touched by the benevolence of life, I thought that matter had assumed concrete form in my person through some fortuitous combination. I thought I was in a position to do good to someone, I felt necessary to the harmonious existence of the universe.

Then I fell in love with Cornelia, a student of French literature. I wooed her for a year, I went with her to cafés, to concerts. Until one day I discovered that once lessons were over the gentle fawn, with her big eyes and curly brown hair, was going to the home of a famous tenor with the Opera to make love to him. This was the start of the corruption of everything, including my magnificent dental arches. Seeing me pale, absorbed and drenched in sweat, my father got worried.

'It isn't the first time you've been in love,' he said. 'Why are you in such distress this time?'

'Because my first wisdom tooth has erupted.'

'Surely wisdom would suggest that you don't despair over unrequited love.'

'But I'm despairing about my tooth. About what they call the dental arch!' I exclaimed. I had no wish to reveal my desperation, my painful rebellion against deception and betrayal.

However, even if the row of my teeth had already been attacked by fierce colonies of bacteria, the real massacre occurred during this time, and it began with UL8. Thus I found myself spontaneously supposing that this tooth was in some way connected to a particular form of judgement: moral judgement, the condemnation of everything that I could not hold good and right, and thus of Cornelia as well.

Concerning the fate of UL8 I refer the reader to pages 199 ff., evoking the process, the stupid quarrel that arose around that tooth, now gone, along with all the caries and all the gold that had covered it for years. UL8 ended up in Dr Metzger's bin, and from there probably in the sewers or on the rubbish tip. All I can say is that that peace, that comprehension of things born in me with UL8 did not last long. Light soon made way for darkness. Keeping 'the light' alive in oneself for a long time is very difficult, not to say impossible. The state of grace lasts a very short time, a hundredth, a fiftieth of our lives. As for the rest it would be better to remain silent. And yet it is from the depth of that darkness that we like to speak, and to speak again, as if it were the only world to be described. Which is not to say that that is not the case. But I shall stop here, lest I discredit what I should like to say about the second wisdom tooth, LL8, which emerged exactly a year after the first.

LL8

Beside the description of this event, as painful as giving birth, there was an article in my diary – I have always been a passionate collector of newspaper cuttings – telling of terrible events in Africa. The first day that LL8 finally emerged, in a country in central Africa a hundred children died of hunger, while in the north-eastern part of the continent some thousands of giant warriors were killed by a tribe of pygmies. 'Big men dead in their own blood, small future men dead in their own filth': that was the caption placed under that newspaper article. Clearly, my inclination to pessimism was already becoming apparent. In my body, that wisdom tooth represented critical judgement, because from that point onwards I always associated it with a heartfelt critique of man's fate on earth. 'Sometimes pessimism is the only salvation,' my father used to say. LL8, which is to say the lower left eight tooth, lasted longer than all the rest. Tucked away in the remotest corner of the oral cavity, where the eye can barely reach, LL8 survived all the storms of my life almost unscathed. Only on two occasions was it on the point of becoming diseased. The first coincided with the day I met Elisabeth, a student of literature: the flesh that enveloped the roots swelled up to cover the occlusal surface, as if the tooth had wished to turn back, beneath the gums, to the prenatal state, to the limbo from which it had come. But perhaps that flesh represented Elisabeth's beautiful arms.

Elisabeth was famous for having participated, five years earlier, in an international youth conference, and for having been among the first to be sent to a country in Central

America, where an exciting popular revolution had installed
a new political order. She was a girl of medium height, quite
plump, with big dark eyes, smooth hair and cheeks that were
always pink. Those cheeks, apart from her large maternal
breasts, were her greatest attraction, giving the impression of
indestructible health, a freshness and an enthusiasm suggested
even by her voice, which was deep and mature. Her clear dic-
tion, free from uncertainties, could be heard ringing out
loudly even in the middle of a great hubbub. I met her in the
reading room of the National Library and approached her
very cautiously – I didn't dare risk rejection in those days –
and began to woo her. She struck me as very romantic;
tender and serious. Only after I fell in love with her did
Elisabeth reveal that she was already engaged. 'I am fond of
you,' she said to me one evening in the old Café Emke, 'but
I'm going to get married to a boy who's just graduated in
engineering. But please believe me when I say that I'll always
be fond of you.'

I fell ill with despair, for days and days I didn't eat, I had a
fever, I couldn't even walk. And yet every evening as I
brushed my teeth I repeated to myself my father's formula: 'I
want to keep my tooth, I want to keep my wisdom.'

During those weeks, as I said, my gums covered LL8, causing me a slight pain every time I closed my jaws. Was it that
wisdom tooth trying to draw my attention to the clouding of
critical judgement by the emotions? Or was it exhorting me
to apply my reason to the passions and the emotions? It was
Kant's *Critique of Pure Reason* that brought me out of that
state of prostration. I was particularly struck by one passage, in
which the great thinker affirms that no emotion, no passion

can unravel its own enigma by the use of pure reason. This can only be achieved through the application of critical judgement, the capacity to contemplate, bit by bit, the way that creation operates, and the reasons for its failures.

I began to analyse my feelings, weighing up each element, each motive, and finally understanding the failure involving Elisabeth and myself. For some mysterious reason, neither of us was sincere with the other. Past lies could not be cancelled out. The failure was irreparable.

To the great relief of my parents, I dedicated myself so thoroughly to the pain of my gums that, little by little, I resumed my studies and my normal life, and after three years I graduated. Then came work and travel all over the world. I forgot all about Elisabeth. Twenty years passed. One day I found myself in London, at Clapham South underground station, where I was waiting for a man who was to give me a parcel, and to whom I was to entrust a small map drawn by my own hand. The stranger, whom my friends had described down to the smallest details of his face and clothing, was late. Suddenly I heard a couple talking in my mother tongue. I turned round and saw Elisabeth on the arm of her engineer.

Blood rushed to my face, all the anger and pain of my stormy adolescent emotions welled up in me. 'How lovely to see you again!' Elisabeth exclaimed, pinker and more enthusiastic than ever. The surprise prevented me from uttering a word.

'Would you come and have dinner with me?' I stammered. 'But of course!' shrieked Elisabeth.

Her husband was equally enthusiastic. 'For three days we've

been eating nothing but meat out of tins. We're just poor tourists, you know. But now we can make up for lost time.'

I invited them to a steak house in the City, spending all the money I was going to use for the rest of my stay. Elisabeth and her husband ate for three. Fortunately, the day after, I was able to meet, at the same time and in the same place, the stranger who, in exchange for my services, resolved my financial problems.

I invited the happy couple to dinner again, took them around some of the sights of London, and then said goodbye with the same feeling of regret that I had experienced on the day of their wedding. The disappointment continued to torment me.

Another year passed and I was transferred to Barcelona. One evening at about ten the phone in my house rang. It was Elisabeth. 'I'm coming on the plane tomorrow. I'll expect you at the airport . . . I hope you'll put me up. You know, I'm not married any more. Since the time I met you in London, I haven't thought about anything but you. See you tomorrow.'

Didn't she care what I felt and thought? Wasn't she interested in the fact that I was married with two children? Critical judgement suggested that I should let her do whatever she liked, but not take her into my home. Had Elisabeth abrogated the right to dominate my life for her own satisfaction? She could go to hell. I was furious but I tried to control myself. That day I brushed my teeth four times, repeating my father's magic formula.

The following day, at the hour suggested by Elisabeth, I went to the airport. From the first light of dawn, LL8 had started hurting again. My cheek was now swollen by an abscess. I didn't understand the exhortation of my tooth, and the moment I saw her arrive, I walked over to her, greeted her and gave her a resounding slap. Then I turned round without saying a word and went back to my car. No one followed me. I turned on the ignition and started driving through the countryside, and after about an hour I returned home to Rachel and the children. I heard nothing more of Elisabeth.

The treatment of LL8 lasted several weeks and Dr Jorge Gelb was paid very handsomely. Before each session I read a few pages of Schopenhauer. To conclude, the molar accompanied me into old age, sitting quietly in its dark corner and, from that moment, feeding my tendency to analyse everything with suspicion, to quibble over every little event, whether external or internal. It didn't even intervene in my final passionate affair with Judith (see p. 211 ff.), or afterwards, in the fog of my old age. It was the final tooth to leave its socket. It too was violently ripped out to make room for a coarse false tooth. By now, critical judgement no longer meant anything to me, the world was no longer of interest. And I stopped caring a long time ago. I am experiencing the rarefied folly of old age with a certain uncritical amusement.

UR8

At this point I must mention UR8, the right wisdom tooth that never emerged. For me it has always represented absence, everything we wait for in vain. But a symbol is a conventional sign, and in this case the sign is absence, non-existence, the void. From the bottom of that void I peep out at UR8. What can I compare it with? I feel dizzy at the mere thought of it,

since the mind would have to turn its attention to this
absolute, irrevocable thing that is in the perfect nothing, to
eternity.

When, once I reached the age of twenty-five, I spoke to my
father about that sense of absence, he heaved a sigh, noisily
sipped two spoonfuls of soup, and then said: 'Wait patiently,
you'll see that it too will emerge one day. Until the end of
time all that will exist is waiting. That's how it will be with
your tooth. If it never comes, if you never achieve final
wisdom, be patient. You will have to be content with what
you have.'

'And what about using a bridge to put in a false wisdom
tooth?'

'I've never heard of a false wisdom tooth. There's already
quite enough fake wisdom in the world,' my father retorted.
'However, you know that I hate all things fake – painted
images, photographs, statues, lyric operas. And false teeth.'

My father, killing animals large and small every day, probably hated everything that belonged to the realm of the senses.
Within me, though, UR8 represented the wisdom of aesthetic judgement which, via the senses – sight, hearing,
touch – can comprehend beauty.

'Everything is based on this deception of the senses, on illu-
sions, on fictions,' Maestro G. said to me one day, years later
in Lodi, after a concert that had received a lukewarm reception. 'Here we have art, beauty, but also, I would say, the
whole man: in deception.'

'Maybe you're being so pessimistic because there weren't
that many people there this evening. The next concert will go
better,' I said.

'No, it's not about that,' he answered. 'The only authentic thing is the feeling of solidarity between the disinherited of the earth. And there's less and less of that. All the rest is "superstructure", as *Das Kapital* puts it, and thus illusion.' The Maestro's handsome face was pale, his ruffled hair dripping with sweat. He had just conducted Beethoven's Seventh Symphony. War had just broken out between China and Vietnam.

During that inauspicious period of my life I found myself in Rome. One August morning an old 'acquaintance' came to see me, to give me an air ticket for Moscow, where I was to accompany my best friend, Maestro G. I knew how important this journey was: in Moscow that great musician, that great man would fall ill, the best doctors would treat him and scrupulously accompany him to his death. I was sure of their plan to kill him. I wondered why. The Maestro couldn't be suspected of betrayal. On the other hand, I knew what my refusal to go with him would mean. There was no choice. I fell into a state of terrible despair. What was to be done? Was life really so sinful? Did the heart of man harbour nothing but betrayal and bestial appetites? Did friendship, mutual esteem and love no longer exist?

One night I dreamed, curiously, that UR8 had emerged into my mouth. I woke up, and with my tongue I began to explore the space in which UR8 should have appeared. The tip of my tongue was so impressed by the dream that it thought it could feel the new tooth, the tooth of missing judgement, missing wisdom. I rejoiced! 'There it is!' I said out loud, in the room of the hotel where I was staying. I ran to the bathroom to look at myself in the mirror. There it was!

My wisdom tooth was born! I was forty years old, and finally the thing I had been waiting for had come about. The world had been redeemed. To hell with everyone who had asked me to take Maestro G. to the slaughter! I had decided to resist, to die. Everything had a meaning for me now. Life and death, nothing and everything had coincided. I spent a few weeks euphoric with an overwhelming sense of trust in the world. My life had ceased to be an uncontrollable chaos: all of a sudden every event seemed to mean something, to act as instruction and sustenance for me. My tongue, my eyes were witness to the fact that my wisdom tooth, my tooth representing aesthetic judgement, existed. I wanted to tell someone of the 'miracle'.

I went to see Dr Fischer and told him what had happened.

'You're a genuine rarity. A terrific example of humanity to show the students. But are you sure of what you're saying?'

'Of course I am,' I answered, 'I've felt it with my tongue, I've checked it with my eyes. It exists, it exists, there's no doubt of that.'

'Show me your mouth,' he said. He began to count the teeth of the upper right arch and looked me in the eyes. 'There are only seven there,' he said gravely.

'Seven?'

'Yes,' he answered. 'Why, didn't you count them? The eighth, the wisdom tooth, hasn't come through.'

In my enthusiasm I hadn't counted my teeth, trusting instead in my dream. Then I remembered a saying that I had learnt from the old temple cantor when I was a child. 'The just man never sleeps.' Small and inexperienced as I was then, I had thought that the maxim was false and tyrannical.

'Really? What would man be without his nocturnal dreams?' I had gone around repeating for years. Now the weight of that maxim rebounded on me, my universe collapsed. 'I don't want to dream any more, I'm going to give up sleeping. My senses, my brain can no longer delude me with their games. My father was right: painted images, music, fictions, beauty are nothing but eternal waiting, eternal absence,' I inwardly declared.

Of course, dreams continued to persecute me for a while longer, until memory began to lose bits of reality. When I was about fifty-five, I found I was failing to recognize the faces of people I knew, names had to be repeated dozens of times. In the morning I couldn't remember the dreams I knew I had had during the night. Had I, then, become a 'just' man?

Surely not. I was simply approaching the day of reckoning. My failing senses, by now as unreliable as imagination, and that absent tooth that had never appeared, were the great void in the miserable mechanism that was my 'self'. 'Waiting and illusion are the destiny of man,' I wrote in my diary.

As to the destiny of Maestro G., the reader will soon find out about that.

LR8

It erupted when I was twenty-four, the very day before my state exam. The previous weeks had passed amidst atrocious pains in my maxilla, which risked compromising my studies, my preparation, and even my recent acquaintance with Rachel: the spectacle of my physical suffering was hardly inviting for a future wife. But Rachel was immediately flooded by a maternal feeling towards me, in the name of which she would torture me for decades. Only late in life, when the 'she-dog' had finally left me, did I learn to tame that trait of the female character (see p. 157 ff.). But let's return to the state exam.

By now resigned either to passing the test by twisting and turning beneath the eyes of the commission, or to withdrawing by showing a medical certificate, the morning of the day preceding the great event I awoke with an unusual sense of well-being. The pain had gone, and I felt filled with a holiday freshness. My mother attributed this 'miracle' to the force of her prayers.

'Yesterday I went to the community and gave them a tidy sum for a school to be rebuilt. The Eternal One listened to me.'

My father smiled. 'I was the one who saved you, by dedicating the slaughter of ten lambs to you,' he confided five years later while we took a short stroll.

Whatever the truth, in a few hours I had run through all my subjects again, and the morning afterwards I went to the exam whistling the final chorus of *Fidelio*, 'Oh, what joy, what joy divine'. Arriving at the place that many people considered a torture chamber, as happy as if I was about to enter a garden of earthly delights, I came away with my best mark for the whole course, and obtained the right to pursue my studies at university. I had been declared a perfect materialist (those courses allowed no other forms of thought) and the fact that the tooth had come through the day before the exam confirmed me in my conviction that I was ready for that philosophical approach to life. I had an explanation for all phenomena. Thanks to the dialectic, in other words the confrontation of two movements or tendencies, this did not surprise me in the least. The whole of life, including art, science and faith, was a massive superstructure, and the spirit was matter's self-reflection.

This certainty troubled me for thirty years, since nothing is more worrying than certainties. One day, an English friend came to Clapham South – he always chose the same station for his meetings – clutching a small volume. It was Berkeley's *Three Dialogues*, a genuine distillation of poison.

'I don't think it's for you,' my friend said with polite solicitude.

'Why not?' I asked, almost offended.

'It would bore you. They're abstract speculations. We seem so pragmatic, but sometimes our philosophy is as far removed from life as Mars from Pluto.'

'If you'll allow me, though, I'd like to take a look at your little book.'

'Be my guest. If you like I'll lend it to you for a few days. But remember that Berkeley was Irish, so he's an original for us English as well.'

Who would ever have thought that the work of a seventeenth-century philosopher could become a weapon of the Intelligence Service? And yet that's what happened. Today I'm convinced that the little volume was delivered to me deliberately to eliminate me from the Party. The idea of playing a double game disturbed them. By causing the collapse of my materialist faith, they were convinced they could win me over to their cause. And it was true that reading that irrefutable demonstration of the non-existence of all material substance destroyed my materialist faith. No one could contradict the iron logic, the elegance, the thrilling superiority of those pages.

'What are we made of, then?' I wondered, after reading it. 'Of the same substance as dreams?' But dreams had already proved poisonous. 'Then what, for Berkeley, is that frail and ferocious creature that calls itself man?' I called my English friend, inviting him to dinner in an Indian restaurant.

'Did you like Berkeley?' my friend asked, staring into my eyes.

'Yes,' I replied resolutely.

'Does that "yes" refer to something practical?' he pressed me with a smile.

I had to tell him which camp I had opted to support, I had to tell him whether I was now on his side or whether I preferred to serve two masters.

'Where no material substance exists, nothing practical exists,' I answered.

We ate in silence. Every now and again my friend stared at me. At the third forkful of some excellent curry and pilau rice, a sudden, tremendous pain shot through LR8, my final wisdom tooth. With the rice I had chewed a small stone, which I spat out along with half of the tooth, split vertically in two.

Throwing me a glance of cruel satisfaction, my friend said: 'You didn't want to make a decision, and you've been punished for that. You will carry the mark of your duplicity as long as that cursed tooth lasts.'

'And you will bear the mark of your stupidity as long as you live,' I yelled, weeping with pain.

A devotee of Freud might argue that I had known perfectly well of the presence of the pebble, and that was why I wanted to bite it. One might maintain that I made the presence of the pebble coincide with my philosophical doubts (Jung's theory of synchronicity). Someone else might suggest that the pebble was the material manifestation of my mental state. I don't know what to think. At a distance of many years, all I know is that these new dental expenses drew Rachel's reproaches down upon my head.

'You could have paid more attention. You know the children need new coats!' she exclaimed irritably when she saw me in misery. After that she accompanied me to see Dr George Steiner, and started haranguing the specialist about his bill.

'If you believe in the values of your nation, if you admit the force of Berkeley's thought, then lower your fee. Berkeley has been the ruin of that tooth,' she said.

Steiner, although originally from Austria, was a great British patriot. Rachel had hit the nail on the head, and the dentist reduced his prices to a more modest level.

Restored by Dr Steiner, LR8 continued to hold out in my mouth for a long time, witness to my 'vertical' division between materialism and its opposite. I have always hated man for being a creature made of clay, while at the same time I have always admired him for that very reason. But I also love him and hate him for the opposite reason, for his spirituality. As to my English friend, I never wanted to see him again. And in any case, some years later I withdrew from all

Party activity. After my retirement I devoted myself for a time to the distribution of books to state organizations. After the great changes around the world I devoted myself to the rearing of Chinese worms, and for years I worked for a student who earned so much money at this business that he became one of the country's first capitalists.

UR1

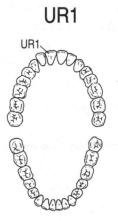

How I lost my first upper right incisor

'We've got another half hour before we have to leave,' said Maestro G. 'I've just got time to run through the *William Tell Overture.*' He was very agitated, fearing the judgement of the Russian audience. I don't know how he avoided fear of the death that lay in wait for him.

'Is it possible that an artist, so absorbed in the practice of his profession, can so lose his feeling for the world?' I wondered. I was really suffering on his account, I didn't know what to do to save him from that journey to Moscow, the equivalent for him of capital punishment.

'You see here, this baton with the luminous tip was given to me in Prague,' the Maestro said with a smile. 'It has something to do with the Black Theatre they have there.' He lifted the baton off the score and started waving it around. We were in a little room in the Hotel Excelsior in Rome. It all struck me as pointless and ridiculous: the shadow of murder fell on everything. I could already see the Maestro stretched out on a hospital bed, the doctor on the point of injecting him with the lethal poison, his body thrown into a coffin and buried in a common grave.

'Check that you've got the air tickets,' the Maestro said calmly.

'Wouldn't it be better to cancel the concert?' I said in a desperate attempt to hold him back.

'What on earth are you thinking about?' he asked, staring at me with big bovine eyes just like those of Socrates, as described by Plato.

'You've had to get things together in a terrible hurry. You're probably not ready.'

'I've always been ready,' he answered. 'It isn't every day you're asked to conduct a concert in Moscow. I've been waiting for this day all my life. I'm a mediocre conductor, you know that, don't you?'

'But what are you saying, Maestro?'

'Yes, that's how it is, and this is a great occasion for me. The rest is silence.'

He was ready to sacrifice his life for that concert. He knew the danger and he was ready to die. So what was more important to him? The idea for which he worked in secret – or art? Or perhaps both to the same degree but not in the same way? I couldn't allow his sacrifice, especially since I had to accompany the sacrificial lamb – in this case my only friend, the only person I revered unreservedly – to the slaughter.

While he was going through the score, I clung to any remaining arguments that might dissuade him. His absorbed expression told me that any attempt would be in vain. When he got up and I helped him into his raincoat, it was a solemn and irrevocable moment for me. We were about to face the ultimate journey.

'Are they going to come and get us?' asked the Maestro when we were in the street. 'I hope they'll let me conduct the concert,' he added.

'No, they don't come and collect anyone here. Let's take a taxi to the airport.'

In those days in that city, invaded by the chaos of millennia, the traffic was unbearable. All of a sudden an idea came to me, a last, desperate attempt to reach safety. If I were to push the Maestro under a car, thus ensuring that he fractured his legs and his arms, I would be rescuing him from the claws of his assassins. I started to study the passing cars. I only had a few minutes at my disposal, just time for the taxi to take us to the nearest station. I mentally measured the speed and dimensions of the vehicles. I certainly didn't want to kill Maestro G. out of an excess of zeal. When I thought the right moment had come, pretending to turn round, I gave him a shove with my elbow and the case I was carrying. The Maestro lost his balance just as a small Italian car was passing, and he was hurled to the ground, and dragged along for a few yards. It was a horrible spectacle, that body rolling around, the blood coming from the torn skin of his face, from his hands, his legs. His shoes flew away, the bag with the score in it ended up under the wheels, and a chilling crunch of bone made the scene look like the end of the world. I felt like weeping.

The Maestro remained motionless for a moment. Then, while the driver was getting out of his car and lots of people were running over, my friend got to his feet, somehow managed to gather his arms and legs together, took a step towards me and gave me a tremendous punch in the face. Through the green and blue lights transmitted to my brain by my sensory organs, I saw the Maestro wobble absurdly before collapsing again on the cobbles in a pool of his own blood. Someone dragged me into the foyer of the hotel. Then I fainted as well. I found myself in bed in the room at the Cultural Institute. My mouth was swollen and painful. With my tongue I explored my oral cavity, and felt my upper right incisor broken in half. Reality had taken hold again.

I was repatriated. I knew that the Maestro's injuries and fractures meant that he would have to spend four months in hospital. He was safe for the moment, and he owed his safety to me. Years later, as we will see, he repaid my kindness by trying to kill me.

Dr Sperber repaired my tooth with a cheap, porous and yellowish polymer. The idea of the aesthetic was alien to that old dentist's mentality: for Dr Sperber the important thing was that everything should work. And thus he ruined UR1 which, after two subsequent repairs, was finally extracted by Dr Taussig, who was unstinting in his bitter criticism of his colleague's work.

'The more you want everything to function, the more chaos you attract,' said the small bewhiskered dentist with the gold-rimmed glasses, the living image of cleanliness and order and thus, if one shared his opinion, of imminent catastrophe.

UL3

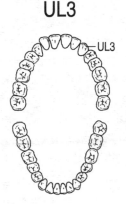

UL3

The first time I dreamt about losing my teeth I was about thirty. I had been fired by the State Import-Export Company, and after some months of uncertainty I had been appointed director of a firm devoted to the global distribution of my nation's arts and crafts. It was my last chance.

One night – my son Gerson had been born three days previously – exhausted by the business of the day, I fell asleep fully dressed on the sofa. In my dream I felt with my tongue that UL3, the upper left canine, was wobbling back and forth, as some of my milk teeth had done many years earlier when I was a child. I gripped the canine between my index finger and my thumb and was stunned to discover that I could slip it easily from my gums, away from its sheath of bone and flesh. Then I repositioned it, and the canine implanted itself solidly in my jaw. 'How strange!' I thought and, still incredulous, repeated the entire operation as hesitantly as I had done a moment before. I woke up with a sense of contentment mingled with anguish, along with the thought that the canine might one day drop out of its socket unbeknownst to me and fall into my soup or the dust of the street. I was also afraid that I might inadvertently swallow it, perhaps while drinking my morning coffee. But then the saltiness of my gums reminded me of the taste of my wife Rachel. Some months later, once Gerson had assumed the appearance of a real human being, the dream was repeated, and the distress, mixed with pleasure, began to return.

I attempted an interpretation of that nocturnal vision, probing the possible psychological meanings and taking note, with a sense of superiority, of the divergence of opinions that exists on the matter. A year later, the dream came true in quite dramatic circumstances. I was in a major city in northern Italy, accompanying a large consignment of dolls and bottles of spirits destined for the Italian market. There was a great deal of agitation in that foggy yet cordial city. A man had fallen from the window of the police station, dying on the spot, and some people held the country's intelligence service responsible. And a short time previously, a bomb had exploded in a Milanese bank, killing thirteen people.

We dined in the best restaurants of the city. One evening, after eating, I noticed, passing my tongue over my lower molars, that the edges of my gums had risen, partially covering the masticatory surface of those teeth. Whilst brushing them that evening, I made the unpleasant discovery that a great deal of blood was coming from my mouth: my gums were painful and sore; their inflammation worried me.

'What could it be?' I asked a company official who was travelling with me. 'What do you think it is?'

'As far as I know, the gums only react like that in cases of syphilis or certain forms of leukaemia. I hope it isn't anything of that kind,' he said.

I became terribly worried. 'I'm done for,' I thought. I felt myself shrinking, I was pervaded by a terrible weakness, my body was losing weight from one minute to the next until it almost lost substance. I felt defenceless, marked, close to complete destruction. I was ashamed of my imminent death.

'Is it certain that it's as my friend said?' I asked the doctor I consulted the following day.

'Certain?' he asked in turn. 'Nothing is certain in this life, not even . . . not even . . .'

Dr Ernesto Weiss, who had emigrated to Israel before finally moving to Italy, lowered his voice. 'Why should we always think the worst? Our people have that tendency, it's true, and it's probably also true that pessimism is the most constructive attitude, but in your case it's a simple inflammation.'

'What kind of inflammation?' I asked, both relieved and at the same time prostrate with uncertainty.

'The name of the illness is periodontitis, and I must tell you that in many cases it involves the premature and inevitable loss of all the teeth.'

'Am I going to lose them all?'

'Yes, inevitably.'

'How long will it take?' I asked, suspended between hope and despair.

'Fifteen or twenty years.'

My sense of self-esteem in my physical appearance, my personal integrity was irreparably humiliated in that moment. 'I'd be better off dead,' I thought, 'rather than being reduced to a defenceless monster.' But soon I was inspired by another idea which almost restored my self-confidence. 'It doesn't matter. When all my teeth have fallen out I'll get myself a nice set of dentures. I'll have false teeth implanted in my jaw. Man can't be reduced so easily to one of those grotesque masks drawn by Leonardo. Rather than being imprisoned in our desolation, we can use the resources of our intelligence. Remember this, if you are ever tempted to yield to despair!' Yes, I dared to challenge my destiny, or Evil, or perhaps simply naked existence, and was repaid in kind: with a challenge.

Dr Ernesto Weiss described the course of the illness to me, explaining that it involved a hereditary component about which nothing could be done, and one that depended entirely on me, on the attention that I devoted to the care of my gums and teeth.

'You have neglected and maltreated them, and yet they are part of you, of your body, with which you live on earth, at least for the time being.'

So the responsibility was mine. Beyond the mysterious perspective of such declarations I sensed a poignant truth. 'The mechanism in which we are enclosed is far from perfect,' I thought, 'we must devote continuous care to it. What can it all mean? We are condemned not to death, but to the imperfection of our body: one is stronger, the other weaker. If the ability to withstand pain, to withstand disease, is inscribed within our body, where then is our freedom of choice?'

None the less, over the years that followed, I dedicated myself, ten minutes a day, five in the morning and five in the evening, to the care of my teeth. I learned to use silk thread to penetrate the gaps, to perform decongestant ablutions, and to run the brush along my gums in such a way as to insinuate the fibres beneath the 'pockets' that form between the flesh and the bone. Despite all this, after two or three years, the neck of UL3, the canine of which I had taken such care, proved to be diseased and blackened. My son, when I smiled at him, burst out laughing. 'Ugh!' he would say.

Rachel, taking advantage of the fact that I had been fired from the company exporting our country's folk art, and thus of the interruption in my constant travels, fixed an appointment with Dr Grossmann, who had opened a surgery on Aurora Street. 'You've got terrible halitosis. You've got to do something,' Rachel whispered to me one night, putting her head on my chest. I didn't trust Dr Grossmann, being worried by his confidence and joviality and also by his coarse hands, his dry skin. When, on the day of my visit, he announced that the neck of the canine was decaying and required a filling, and that I also needed a 'general clean', I was frightened and decided not to keep the next appointment.

On my own initiative I began to perform simple ablutions with Odol. One of those nights I fathered Leah, and my father, the local *Schächter*, was particularly delighted. When I left for Hamburg to take up a two-year post at the Finno-Ugric Institute of Language and Literature, he took in my wife and children.

The first 'general clean' and the filling of the carious neck
were carried out in the surgery of Dr Bernheim, on
Möwestrasse, in the city centre. The woman dentist whose
task it was to remove the yellowy-green deposits of tartar, of
crystallized food stuck between the teeth, was a young
Romanian, whom everyone in the dental clinic called Dr
Angela. She was extremely beautiful: her short red hair
emphasized the strong, regular features of her face. She had a
light and harmonious way of walking, her hands moved my
head with faint little touches, but during our first session she
began to hook away at the tartar so energetically that she
made me weep with pain, and it was through my tears that I
saw the intensity of her gaze. Her eyes were grey-blue, large
and round, her eyebrows fine and arched, and her gaze, fixed
on the inside of my mouth, displayed a level concentration
that I had never seen in anyone before.

'She's looking at the refuse, the detritus of life. How, then,
will she look at my soul?' I wondered.

Dr Angela proved unwilling to talk to me about anything
other than oral hygiene. 'Be patient,' she repeated every now
and again, pushing, pulling, scratching my teeth. I wept
uncontrollably. 'Don't despair,' she said once, 'there are worse
things in life: illness, hunger, thirst, old age.' She was hurting
me, the pain had spread throughout my whole head, and I
could think of nothing but my suffering. One time she
stroked my cheek, tenderly. 'Poor thing,' she said, 'I must
have touched the lachrymal sac. Who knows how you'll cry
when you have a real reason to? We all have to endure great
pain in our lives, it would be awful otherwise.'

She whispered those words to me in a tone of objectivity

mixed with indifference, making me wonder if she realized that she was literally torturing me, and if she knew of the efforts that I was making to withstand it: I continued with my defiance. At the end of the session I spoke to her about it. 'Yes, yes,' she said incredulously. For her, pain was the stuff from which life was cut, the backdrop of being, the music of the spheres. I was sorry when the treatment came to an end.

'I hope I'll see you again,' I said, removing the paper and plastic towel that the dentist had draped over me. It was our final session, the May afternoon was still.

'Perhaps we'll see each other again,' the dentist said. 'While you still have some of your teeth there's always the possibility that we might see each other. From now on I'm going to be based in Hamburg, my husband is working here.'

The slight tone of bitterness that I thought I heard in her voice encouraged me to ask her if I could see her that evening, or on one of the evenings that followed. She didn't say no, but she did specify that Mr Maurer, her husband, a businessman, would have to come along too. We met in the large restaurant on the lake, the usual place for such rendezvous. We drank tea and ate pastries.

'You see, I've made you cry, I've hurt you, but, in one sense at least, the pain of absence is much more intense than the pain of something, some organ that is still alive and present, like a limb, or the heart, or the teeth.' Angela smiled with her beautiful lips, which that evening were painted a gaudy red.

'The dentist is wrong,' I thought, 'the pain of absence is attenuated after a while, man gets used to everything.' To be honest, I've never known till now whether I consider that faculty to be beneficial, or man's worst defect, but what I do know is that being separated from Dr Angela immediately filled me with a painful sense of deprivation. Thereafter we entered into a very long correspondence which was only interrupted recently, after my last molar left me. I learnt from her letters that during what is generally known as the Second World War Angela lost all her relations, who died under the poison gas that came from the showers in a so-called extermination camp. For decades, the faces of her parents and her older brothers and sisters reappeared in her dreams, their words echoed around her brain, as if no time had passed. Absence was the sign of our love, expressed, even in its physical manifestations, only in letters. Angela managed to describe the smell of her body to me, and asked me to do the same. The agony of absence was the only real pleasure in her life: for me, of course, it was only agony. Even now, wearing a shoddy prosthesis, I find myself thinking about my teeth again – and about Angela – and for the same reason I wrote down their story in the hope of easing the suffering caused by their loss, a profound feeling similar to that which one experiences when one thinks about death.

I shall stop talking about the upper left canine. After the 'general clean', Dr Bernheim, the owner of the clinic, filled the caries in the neck of the tooth personally. I refused the injection and faced the drilling and the preparation of the Black's cavity without so much as a groan, tensing all my muscles to the point of stupefaction. A desperate cry for help arose from my consciousness and ran along the trajectory of the pain. My whole being was contained in that cry, and it must have reached its target, because I emerged unscathed from the operation, while the intensity of the pain made me think that I was close to death. I ended up with the neck of the canine incredibly white and smooth. The treatment was not expensive, and for many years it saved that tooth, which, as time passed, began to lengthen immeasurably.

Every now and again, almost unconsciously, I would stop in front of a mirror, raising my upper lip with my index finger, and look at the state of my canine. I hadn't the courage to contemplate it for more than a few seconds. But in this way I was able to observe the inexorable retreat of the gums and the bone, until one day it seemed to me that UL3 could fall out at any moment. Still the tooth remained in its socket for a little longer, in all its equine length. When I was around fifty-five it began to move slightly, and then the dream I had had a short time earlier suddenly came true: one morning, almost painlessly, the canine slipped out. But it would not be reimplanted – in that respect my dream had deceived me – as I realized with that sense of shame when we actually experience events we have foreseen.

So now I am awaiting the revelation of the one true dream, with all the pain and the terror that goes with it: the dream of death. For ages I wept over the loss of UL3, because it was Angela who left me with that tooth, and I have never managed to get used to its loss.

Five years ago, when I told Angela – by letter, of course – of the loss of the tooth, she suddenly did something she had never done in all the previous years; she called me on the phone. She told me that her letters had had only one purpose: to obtain my replies and, one day, to be able to burn them, destroying those beautiful memories at the same time. To look at the flames would be the greatest pain of her life, just as I had been her greatest love. She reminded me in a whisper of something that I had once written to her: that as a boy, during the war, I had for weeks eaten nothing but a piece of dry bread with the addition of a little tomato purée. Sucking the tubes of tomato concentrate has remained one of my few real pleasures, just as the loss of the things she held most dear had been for her. I remember her weeping while the words that I had written to her turned to ash. The telephone made the sound of her voice even more painful to endure.

That evening I burned her letters as well, and wept as only a toothless and rather absent-minded old man can weep. It was not the feeling of loss that caused those belated tears, but the revelation of an unavoidable human state: sans eyes, sans teeth, sans everything. Anything else is illusion.

LR1

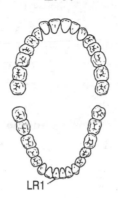

LR1

In almost sixty years, my first lower right incisor has never undergone alterations of any kind. While its neighbour LL1 was the spy upon the vicissitudes of my life, this tooth has always remained extraneous to the rest of my life. However, the day on which eight teeth were extracted to make room for dentures, just at the moment when LR1's turn arrived, I thought, as if in a moment of inspiration, of Maestro G., the man who had always had such an influence on me. I saw him again on the podium of the Great Hall of the Academy, busy conducting the *Leonora* Overture no. 3. He was very young, considering how famous he was. I recalled the dedications he had written on my programmes at various concerts over a

period of thirty years. It was our secret means of communication. I pretended to ask him for an autograph, and he wrote
messages in code. I have kept some of them in the bottom of
my drawer.

'Othello will die tomorrow,' was one mysterious note. The
following day a famous politician from southern Europe,
whose name was reminiscent of Othello, died.

'The man will not live,' was another message, and subsequently in Russia an important member of state died, whose
name echoed the Greek word for 'man'.

Yet another was menacing in its content. 'Music tolerates
no faithlessness. It avenges itself through silence. It is silent
about revenge.'

We also had another kind of code, of course. If, before raising his arm to bring in the orchestra, he scratched behind his
ear, I knew I had to phone him; when he held one hand in
the pocket of his smoking jacket and flicked through the score
with the other, it meant that a negotiation was underway;
when he smoothed his hair before starting to conduct a passage, it meant that my message was unclear (it had as many
meanings as there were hairs!). These gestures have been so
ingrained, one by one in my memory, that each of them, as
long as I live, will continue to live in time's gravel bed.

After the experience that had made us mortal enemies, and
after his final disappearance from my life, a few days before the
extraction I received an unexpected little note.

'So you think you are free of Maestro G. for ever? I haven't
managed to get you in this life but I'm not going to give up.
You can never free yourself from your masters.'

When I was thirty, LR1 began to twist sideways somewhat, pushing itself forward in relation to its neighbours. It had remained white. At the precise moment when Dr Metzger, who was preparing to fit my dentures, pulled it from my mandible with a melodramatic gesture, and raised it aloft, all the notes of all the Maestro's concerts echoed in my ears in a single gigantic chord, all the secret messages came to me in a single sign.

UR4

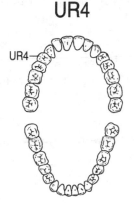

UR4

Of all the individual fates of my teeth, the most curious per-haps was that of UR4, the first upper right premolar. Only after a huge lapse of sixty years did I manage to discover cer-tain coincidences between the story of my mouth's trusty white worker and the events of my generation. One evening, I took a little black notebook, bound in cardboard, from the secret drawer of the old sideboard at home and tried to recon-figure certain jottings that I had for a time been in the habit of making at midnight each evening, using a coded script of my own invention. For reasons that should not be difficult to guess, I burnt that little notebook. First, however, I pulled out some pages on the subject of UR4.

I had lost that tooth a week before in a manner that was unpredictable and, I would say, rather dramatic. But thinking about it afterwards, there was nothing dramatic about the event, it might even have been called ridiculous, because of the intrinsic cruelty of the way it had occurred. I shall relate the manner in which I lost it, after providing a brief summary of the discovery, very important to me, which led me to tell the story of UR4.

Every time a president of the republic or a head of state was killed in some part of the world, UR4 would become diseased. For this reason, with the passing of the years I had christened my premolar the 'presidential tooth'.

It was first repaired on the day of the murder of the president of the greatest power in the western world. On the neck of the tooth a caries of remarkable size had formed, as if a gleaming black beast, such as an ant, was trying to climb that smooth white column. I was studying for a specialist course in foreign politics and working quite hard. I had just met a girl called Martha, and one afternoon I had invited her to a café. Some time later, I looked at myself again in the mirror to check my appearance; it was then that, as I hooked the corner of my mouth with my index finger and pulled it up towards my right ear, I spotted that gleaming, dark stain on the surface of my tooth. I was so horrified by that vision that I wanted to tell Martha not to come and meet me.

In fact the caries was concealed by my cheek, did not disfigure my face, and only a very broad smile exposed it to view. And I didn't smile often. I was a grim and surly boy, with scruffy hair and shirts that could hardly have been described as smart. I couldn't contact Martha, so I was obliged to go and meet her. During our date, which was fairly romantic, I could think only about that terrible ant nestling in my mouth. When the moment to say goodbye finally arrived, I felt a great sense of relief, which Martha noticed. Unable to imagine what could be going on in my mind, the girl was visibly offended, and she refused to go out on a date with me again. The day after this romantic disaster, the flaw was to be repaired – I had gone back to old Lissauer – and I found out about the president's death. Looking at these old notes, I wondered even then what connection there could have been between those two events in the great fabric of universal history.

Eighteen years passed and my doubts deepened. I discovered ever closer connections between what happened within my own body and external events. The day the Egyptian president was killed, by a cannon shot, an enormous hole appeared in UR4, as though a projectile had entered the tooth. Of course, the colony of bacteria that provoked the caries had been lying in the palatal wall of UR4 for a long time, but its collapse occurred that very day.

I returned to Dr Stadler on Acacia Street to repair the enormous caries, as if to attempt to compensate for the bloody murder of the president who had tried, in some way, to restore peace to that region of the world, which even then was afflicted by decades of wars large and small.

Peace was achieved, and the filling held for some years. I was almost certain that my new dentist's magnificent work would last until my death when a pistol shot suddenly caused it to fall out. Of course the shot was not aimed at me, nor was it fired in my country. I only established the relationship between the assassination of the Swedish president and the loss of the filling when I found my notes, but I remember that in those days I had had some suspicions in that direction. Just what it was that linked my premolar to the assassination of the president of one of the most orderly and peaceful countries in the world, I have never worked out, just as I have never discovered the motives for that crime. And yes, I have sought to obtain information about it, from colleagues and opponents in my uneasy profession. Had I been better acquainted with the facts, I might perhaps have understood the legacy of my dental inflammations: but all my efforts have proved futile in the end.

Recently it was suggested that an Italian criminal organization was involved in that mysterious crime, which took place in broad daylight. On hearing this, I felt quite ill. 'Might that terrible secret society have been the main cause of my teeth rotting?' I thought. 'They're capable of anything, those people. Who knows, perhaps they're responsible for the streptococci that went on to ruin my mouth.' Anyone could appreciate that idea, since the name of that secret society is linked so often these days to so many of the most grisly mysteries and massacres. But, as I have said, I should have suspected something at the time of the murder. Behind every event there lies another event, I had jotted down in the black notebook. My suspicions then were further reinforced by the fact that when the filling of UR4 was being restored, a resin was used which perfectly imitated the colour of the nicotine that had stained my teeth. Applying that brown resin to imitate something that was already damaged was like giving a man who has always walked with a limp an artificial leg deliberately shorter than his healthy one. An arrogant fiction,

typical of such secret organizations. It goes without saying that
my ruminations are merely the working out of an obsession,
but obsession has often been the driving force behind man's
best deeds as well as his worst, and where it is absent reason
cannot function properly.

But let us return to UR4. A few weeks after I met Livia –
I was already over fifty – I decided to have the tooth capped.
I had been blessed, despite so many changes of fortune and so
many different jobs, with a smile, at once sly and disen-
chanted, which was similar to that of some of the famous men
born in my district to families like my own. I wanted at all
costs to remain true to that smile which Livia had discovered,
and to the international celebrities (photographers, actors,
writers) that she suggested as my possible doubles. I very
much liked that role, I liked that smile. To make it truly daz-
zling, I thought at first to have UR4 covered with gold, as I
had done with UL8 and UL7. But then, after the collapse of
my stormy affair with Livia, I opted for porcelain. I made an
appointment with Dr Sperber, the successor to Dr Stadler,
who had been caught asking neighbours and acquaintances
for the dirty nappies of newborn babies. ('I have to rebuild my
bacterial flora,' he said, 'a course of streptomycin has exter-
minated all my bacteria. I have to eat baby poo every day,
spread on some bread.' For giving vent to this particular
passion, he was deserted by all his clients, and even reported to
the police.) Dr Sperber, when he came to replace Dr Stadler,
subjected the surgery on Acacia Street to three days of disin-
fection. I was about to visit him when I learned that a revolver
had been fired at the Turkish prime minister. I didn't dare
touch the presidential tooth, who knows what other disasters

I might have caused. I left it alone and for some years nothing happened.

The filling in UR4 fell out suddenly during the funeral of our former prime minister, hanged thirty-three years previously and, after some political changes, rehabilitated one fine day. The word sounded truly ridiculous in context, because what purpose could a dead person serve if not that of being dead? In fact, at such funerals, the coffin contained nothing but some strip of rotting flesh found in a common grave. The great crowd that had mustered sang the praises of the idea personified at one time by the man to whom those pieces of decaying flesh had once belonged. That truly macabre ritual had nothing to do with such ideals. I too was present at the event and, contemplating the contents of the coffin, my tongue distractedly went in search of the old filling of UR4: it wasn't there, just as the prime minister wasn't in the coffin. Pushing through the crowd I left and ran to Dr Sperber. After three days of the most exhausting sessions, UR4 was encapsulated in porcelain. Rachel told me I looked like a different man since at this point my smile was once again beginning to desert me.

These are the last two steps, and the dramatic finale.

UR4 did not seek to add a great deal to the death by firing-squad of the Romanian president and everything that followed in Europe, only sending out the occasional sudden and inexplicable twinge. One night five years ago I dreamt about the famous and tyrannical head of a large eastern nation, now broken down into little independent states. 'Man of steel' he had been called by his companions in arms. In the dream he wanted to explain to me how he had died and he was walking towards me. I dodged him abruptly, and woke up jerking my head away from my pillow. I banged my right cheek against the edge of the little chest of drawers. The bump was terrible, extremely painful. I yelled with all my strength and Rachel, rolling towards me, put my head on her breast and stroked it. Her nightdress turned red: a lot of blood was coming out of my mouth. UR4 had split, the tooth was moving, and I had a lot of grazes on my face. We went to the hospital, and some days later to Dr Sperber, who, with much regret, had to extract the premolar. I said goodbye to the illusion of history. I knew I was ultimately alone, and that I would have to walk the tightrope of pain, from start to finish. Yes, now the rope was pulled tight.

UL1 AND UL2

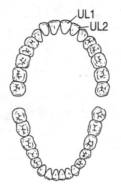

The two incisors of my upper left dental arch came as a terrible surprise to me: it was through them that I discovered that the whole of life is riddled with holes all the way through. My theory is the product of the slow and gradual elaboration of a thought, but also of a flash of inspiration. I was twenty-five years old when Dr Lubetzki, during a meticulous inspection with a very fine probe, discovered the caries that had insinuated itself into the distal surface of my finest tooth. Looking at old photographs, in which I display a smile worthy of the greatest actors of the day, I see a brilliantly white set of teeth and four incisors of pearly perfection. In those days, despite that smile, I had little confidence in my external appearance,

and considered myself decidedly ugly. Today, the boy who
appears in those pictures strikes me as truly seductive. The
idea that I might have been like that consoles me, but it also
makes me melancholy. Why is it that we can never value ourselves for what we are?

To return to my incisor, it was my annual visit to the late
Dr Lissauer's surgery that revealed its diseased state. A little
black dot, spotted by good old Lissauer in his concave mirror,
bore witness to the beginning of the caries. Working with
the fissure bur, the dentist enlarged that tiny cavity, removing
all the caries. Then he put a disinfecting agent into that
round grotto and asked me to come back in two days' time.
It was the first time that, instead of amalgam, a resin by the
name of Starlet was put in my mouth. Looking in my mouth
at home with the help of my mother's little mirror, I saw that
in place of the hole that had been made in the two contigu-
ous teeth there was a little white protuberance: the filling was
robust.

Two years later, I was spending the evening with Esther, my
lover at the time. Leaving the Fisherman's restaurant, we
walked towards the castle and romantically abandoned ourselves to long and passionate kisses. All of a sudden I felt a taste
of ether in my mouth and, pulling away from Esther, became
aware that my breath was slicing through my gums like a
blade. Immediately my tongue began to probe the spot where
I had discovered an inconsistency. Sure enough, between the
two left incisors there was a hole; the filling had fallen out,
probably sucked out by my breath, and now it was lying in the
depths of someone's stomach, either my own or Esther's.

I could no longer look Esther in the eye and, setting off by her side, I walked her home. It was cold, and the wind was stronger than usual for the season.

'What's wrong?' Esther asked me, seeing me staring into the void, my eyes wide open.

'Nothing,' I answered. Then, without knowing why, I said: 'I feel as if I'm riddled with holes. There's a hole through my very being.'

She began to laugh, showing her brilliant white teeth. I was in despair.

The hole in the fine wall of my incisors gave me the feeling my face was a mask, and that through that mask air was rushing through a void. I felt two-dimensional, and terribly exposed to the slightest breeze, like a plant. Until that moment my teeth had served to contain me within myself: as a result of the hole, communication with the outside world made me feel insubstantial to myself. All the more so since I had to tell Rachel ever more barefaced lies at home. It seems silly to attribute such importance to a carious tooth, and yet I felt I was lost. The day after the filling broke I had to set off for Italy, to head a small commercial delegation, as certain secret missions were called in those days. A young politician had been killed in America, Turks and Greeks were arming themselves for the possession of a small island, and the Chinese were occupying China. My colleagues and I went first to Rome and then to Trieste, and it was there that the wind, the famous and terrible Bora, as soon as it entered my mouth, made my idea of myself as a mask full of holes utterly unbearable. While my travelling companions went to take pictures in a little Piedmontese village, near a military base, I flicked through the telephone directory in search of a dentist.

It was thus that I came upon the name of Dr Wiesenfeld, a little old man who was moved to tears at the sound of his own language.

'An M16, or perhaps an M17, please,' he said to the young nurse, after cleaning the round cavity between the two incisors with the bur. 'I'm chiselling away here. Generally I haven't the patience for any of my clients. But you remind me of my youth. When this filling falls out, you'll remember yours too, I hope,' said Wiesenfeld, clapping me on the arm. M17 was a synthetic resin, a polymer the same slightly yellowish colour as my teeth.

'To tell the truth, I prefer amalgam, I'm old-fashioned,' Wiesenfeld declared. 'In amalgam you have matter that is alien to the mouth, but it's not porous, the bacteria can't get into it. Do you want me to follow the dictates of the great Danube school and give you an amalgam filling?'

'No,' I answered, perhaps with excessive haste. 'I'd rather not see that there is a hole there. I'm worried that I'll go on feeling that my entire person is riddled with holes, as I do at the moment.'

'I see you're horrified by the thought of a void. It doesn't bother me any more. I feel utterly resigned to the void or to whatever it is that, perhaps afterwards . . .'

The day that filling fell out I was approaching fifty, and by then I too was resigned. The extraction of three teeth had had the effect of enlarging the space between the remaining twenty-nine, and the two upper incisors of the semi-arch on the left were moving away from each other. The Black's Class II cavity made by Dr Wiesenfeld became enlarged, irregular and jagged. The second time the filling fell out the two caries could no longer be treated together, and UL1 and UL2 were reconstructed one at a time. I had already given up cigarettes and fatty foods by this point, and so, instead of the old resin M17, the two incisors were filled with the new and very expensive ceramic that Dr Schönbaum of São Paulo wanted to use. I was in Brazil to oversee a deal between our company and a local factory, about which I am unable to talk in greater detail. Our field of action, however, was Bolivia and later Chile. While Schönbaum was working my ears were filled, not with the droning of the drill, but with the rumble of armoured cars and Chilean aeroplanes, the screams of prisoners and the wounded, the dark sensation of fatality and suspense that characterizes South American revolutions. All of a sudden I thought of Dr Wiesenfeld, resigned to the void, and of Esther from whom I had parted only because I was ashamed of that tell-tale hole in my mask, in comparison with her own face, which could have appeared on a cameo. One day, Esther, whom I had loved with a confused feeling halfway between humility and exaltation, sent me a photograph of herself from Copenhagen, the city to which she had been transferred. 'So that you can distinguish me from other girls, in your memories.' In the photograph she was very beautiful: tall, prosperous, smiling.

Afterwards, the hole between the two incisors became further enlarged, because the neck of the two teeth was left uncovered by my receding gums. The colour could not be constantly renewed, so for years I carried in my mouth a brown hole hidden by my upper lip: something obscene, like the lower regions of the body. For ten years I dared not smile and, to tell the truth, I didn't much feel like it. The fourth tooth to leave me was that incisor, UL1. To replace it, I had a bridge built, but soon UL2 began to move as well, until my last dentist, Dr Metzger, subjected it to an 'avulsion', thus freeing me from my agonies. By now there was no longer any sense in thinking of myself as something delicate, something exposed to the wind, ephemeral but potentially perfect. In losing my teeth, I had begun to put down roots, paradoxically, like a fat old plant in life's stony desert.

LR2

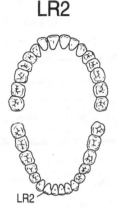

LR2

The day I had LR2 extracted I was barely thirty-five years of age. For two years I had been dependent on the Ministry of Foreign Affairs for my livelihood. I went on missions with a number of commercial delegations, took part in cultural exchanges, organized exhibitions. In Lagos, an English businessman had lent me a Jaguar for a few days, and a few pounds which had allowed me to buy wooden totems and chairs from the local craftsmen. Over the years these became the favourite toys of Gerson and Leah, my two children. For Rachel I had bought some lovely hand-painted fabric, from which she cut dresses that reached down to her feet, as was the fashion in those days. The shape allowed her to hide the rotundity of her body, which had grown heavy with the years and the birth of two children.

The English businessman reappeared some years later, in Argentina, asking me a small favour in return. I didn't deny him. Thus began my friendship, my first true collaboration, with the greatest European Empire, already master of half the world: the United Kingdom. One evening, during a long stay in my homeland (I was studying for a survival course in the equatorial rain forest), the phone rang. It was my father. 'Will you come and see my final slaughter? Remember it's your duty as a son to help your old father.' I couldn't refuse, as, over the years, I had devoted my greatest efforts to coming to terms with his paternal authority and with the awesome symbolic significance attached to my father's trade. The *Schächter*, the ritual butcher, was in my eyes not only the assistant to the angel of death but, equally obviously, the great castrator. My own chaotic relationship with the opposite sex or, simply, with the 'Other' has been greatly influenced by this.

From the first time my father took me into the yellow buildings of the communal abattoir, I became aware of a sense of terror and solemn joy. I felt I was about to witness the sole true event of the universe: death. I was eight years old, and the idea of the instant snuffing-out of my 'ego' made my heart beat frantically, brought a flood of colour to my cheeks, and gave me a sensation of vertigo. Entering the abattoir, the first thing that struck me was the dirtiness of the place, and even today I associate the idea of death with that image of filth. Everywhere there were swarms of flies hovering over excrement, intestines thrown on the cobbled surface of the walkways leading from one shed to the next, piles of bones and puddles of blood. The screams of the pigs and the bleating of the sheep masked the hoarse voices of the butchers, who, wielding great switches, drove the animals towards the place of their execution. My father brought me into a dark shed where, at that very moment, a bull was being led to its death and, batting its eyelashes, apparently ignorant of its fate, was trampling on the head of another bull already severed from its body. At the sight of this, I was filled with fear, I started screaming and ran away. My father caught up with me, put his arms around me and whispered: 'It's nothing, don't be frightened, it's just a sick old bull.'

'If it's so sick why don't they make it better?' I asked.

'We've all got to die when our turn comes,' my father murmured, leading me towards the exit.

That day he bought me a bag of the sweet we call potato sugar, and at Pesach (which was a week away), he sang me the parable of the kid with special, smiling solemnity. The angel of death that kills the butcher was supposed to free me from the fear of my father, since he too in the end was mortal. But rather than relieving me, the idea made my anguish all the worse. 'What are you saying? My father has to die because he slaughtered the cow that drank the water that put out the fire? And who will protect me when my father has been "slaughtered" by the angel of death?' That long chain of killings terrified the life out of me, I was dismayed by the laws of life. Perhaps it was to conquer that terror that I engaged in so many different professions, so many betrayals, even at the expense of poor Rachel and all the women who have crossed my path.

But let's get back to LR2. The day my father invited me to

witness his final slaughter, I had an appointment with Dr
Sperber. The usual inspection of my teeth (I went to the dentist for an annual check-up) had shown that the roots of LR3
and LL3, the two lower canines, were showing dry caries, and
that immediate intervention was required to prevent the
spread of the disease. If I wished to be present at my father's
farewell to his trade, I had to cancel my appointment with the
dentist. That is what I did and, since I would never resort to
bribery or anything of the kind, I had to wait a further two
months to have my teeth treated. I was thirty-five, as I have
said, when for the second time I crossed the threshold of the
communal abattoir on Kerepes Street, asking the way to the
department of ritual slaughter. I found it with some difficulty, among the malodorous outhouses of that terrible place.
In the midst of my life, with a considerable range of experience and reckless commercial and cultural expeditions behind
me, I contemplated once again the spectacle of universal
death, and this time I did not run away.

I greeted my father with a kiss on the cheek, and as I
leaned against him I became aware of the sweetish odour of
blood. I stood somewhat apart and observed the ceremony. A
bullock was led into the cement-floored shed, men bound its
back hooves speedily and in silence and hoisted it up by a
chain. The animal started up a deafening roar, the shed began
to echo with its bellows. Within moments, my father
approached the beast and with a long knife severed its carotid
artery. A tremor ran through the animal's entire body, but it
was unable to move, since ritual practice dictated that its horns
were also fixed to two metal rings driven into the floor. The
life rapidly fled that mass of flesh, while the blood flowing on

to the cement was washed away by powerful jets of water. A life was over, becoming an aggregate of fibres, nerves, bones; a huge, empty puppet. When all the blood had left the bullock's slit throat (the purpose of the rite), the animal was lowered to the ground, and within a few minutes it was cut into pieces by skilful butchers.

All the workers applauded my father and shook his hand, the employees of the community who had come specially to wish him all the best gave him a parchment certificate and introduced him to the new *Schächter*, an enormous, blond, stammering, sweaty young man. The flesh of the bullock was not very different from his own. I couldn't help but see this job as a metaphor for life. I embraced my father, and he, with tears in his eyes, confessed to me that he would miss this horrid place terribly in the years to come. 'Years, months, days, who knows, maybe tomorrow we will have ceased to exist, if that's what is meant for me,' he said. He cleaned his knife, put down his apron, folded it up, put it in a leather bag and went out with me into the open air, into the stench of the rotting innards that lay on the ground, of the excrement, the blood.

The next day, my two lower canines began to hurt: it was not a real pain as such, but what dentists call 'awareness'. LR3, which I identified with music, and LL3, with the erotic instinct – more base, more unmotivated, more canine, more uncouth – had begun to reveal their own necks, showing themselves in their true essence. For a month and a half I was gripped by that awareness, and then Dr Sperber treated the two conditions of music and of carnal lust by filling both teeth at the same time. It was a terrible experience. The drilling made my whole face vibrate. It was as though I was wearing many different masks, and everything was trembling at the same time under the impulse of some infernal machine. I thought I was going mad. The moment Dr Sperber took out the drill it seemed to me that the world was over, emptied, and I fell into a kind of lethargy. That day saw the final, terrible bombing of a small city in South East Asia. Perhaps the vibration of my face and the trembling of the walls of Hanoi happened contemporaneously, or at least that was the analogy I described in my diary. That afternoon the necks of the two canines were coated with a resin identical in colour to my teeth: a bit yellowish, a bit brown, a bit white.

Once LR3 and LL3 were treated, I also seemed relieved of my two obsessions: concerts no longer attracted me as they once had, and as to the baser instincts of sex, I discovered the day after the operation that they were no longer quite so 'carnal'. My underground walk with Agnes (see p. 103 ff.), who had returned to me after a number of years, didn't really excite me. One afternoon I asked for leave from my employers and went with Rachel, without the children, to a place outside the city called Fresh Valley. There we made love with the calmness appropriate to an old married couple. I then set off on a mission to Colombia, and upon my return – a number of months had passed since my session with Dr Sperber – I found that LR2 had shifted oddly backwards. One night, after writing in my diary, while I was looking in the bathroom mirror, I had the notion of manipulating the second lower right incisor between my index finger and my thumb: I was horrified to discover that it moved. It was going to drop out! Expelled from my mouth, exposed to mortality, just as Adam had once been driven out of Paradise. I foresaw the beginning of a long period of shakiness, of progressive enfeeblement, of misery. I ran to Dr Sperber. I asked him if he could prevent the incisor from wobbling with one of those metal appliances that I was starting to see in the mouths of people my age. The doctor said any such attempt would be fruitless: what we would have to do was cover the whole lower arch, because a domino effect had been set in motion. LR3, the canine of Beethoven and Schubert, Vivaldi and Purcell, had leaned to the left, forcing the root of the neighbouring incisor into too precarious a position.

'Bloody music!' I thought. 'What havoc you cause in people's minds and bodies!' But at that moment I understood that music had nothing to do with it: LR2, the incisor adjoining the canine, was in my mouth to represent the death instinct. In the period that had elapsed between the two visits to my father's abattoir, it had begun the process of its own demolition, beginning to cede its own terrain in my mandibular bone to the tooth of music. This was not an inflammation or a caries: LR2 had set the gradual process towards my death in motion. I ran to Dr Lubetzki, whom my father had once more suggested to me, and begged him to extract LR2, to build a bridge and replace the incisor with a prosthesis. I thought that in that way I might be able to bring events to a halt. Dr Lubetzki obeyed me, and extracted LR2 very skilfully.

Three days after that extraction, one June afternoon, my father was found dead in his house on the Transylvania Road (my mother was in hospital with a severe fracture of the femur). My father had been sitting at the dinner table, calmly leaning back against his chair. In front of him a book was open: *Instructions for survival in the equatorial rain forest.* It was a Ministry of Defence publication for the use of the Secret Service. He had asked Rachel if he could borrow it. Perhaps he was planning on getting away from everyone, hiding in the virgin forest, camouflaging himself as an explorer, so that the angel wouldn't find him. Learning of his death – one of his neighbours called me on the phone – I felt an immense pain and an even greater fear: my father's death was really half of my own. Now I was alone with myself, on earth: with myself and with the angel of death, who slaughtered my father, who killed the cow, which drank the water, which put out the fire and so on all the way down to the kid whose Semitic nose – as one famous poet has it – represented, with its bleating, the pain of all living beings on earth.

It was during this time that Maestro G. appeared in my city.

LR6

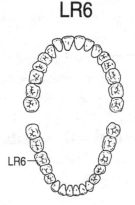

LR6

The first lower right molar was the tooth which was, for me, connected to what is called the chthonic sense of existence. The strength that man draws from the earth I, in the most difficult moments of my life, drew from that tooth, perhaps because it very soon became an image for my life.

I was twenty-eight when LR6 became carious and began to cause me pain. I was working in the castle, at the Museum of National History, and spent hours endlessly watching over old exhibits and naïve paintings of three or four centuries ago, depicting battles, decapitations, solemn oaths. My work ended at five in the afternoon; afterwards I would usually have a coffee in the nearest café, where I would meet up with

Agnes, one of my colleagues. Through a little iron gate whose existence she had brought to my attention, we entered the subterranean passageways of the castle. There we would kiss for hour upon hour, forgetting work, family, friends, time. One spring evening, I emerged from there with my cheeks and jaw in pain. I thought the cause of this ache might have been a draught or the long period of tension in my facial muscles, but after two or three days I realized that this was not the case. I had toothache. To be precise, LR6 had become carious, and now it was doing everything it could to draw itself to my attention. It pulsed, it stung me with sudden twinges until it caused my cheek and gums and possibly even my jawbone to swell.

Responding to this desperate signal, I called Dr Lissauer, asking him to receive me the same day and free me of my pains. In this way I became acquainted with the Bartelemi probe, since Dr Lissauer, after insisting on some swift and painful drilling, used it to inspect the root canals and the root tips of the carious tooth.

'Do you want us to try an avant-garde operation?' he asked, granting me a moment of respite.

'What is it?' I whimpered, both terrified and attracted by the novelty.

'We could delicately remove this tooth, repair the root tips and the canals and then put it back in its place.'

'No!' I shouted and Lissauer, from behind his grey whiskers, smiled.

'Don't shout like that, the operation would hurt you, not me. There's no sense in shouting. Now let's see, though, if there's nothing to be done, I'll put arsenic in the tooth and

next time, with the nerve extractor, I'll remove the source of
the pain, a tiny nerve. But none of it may prove to be necessary. We'll see.'

As for myself, I already regretted saying no to the avant-
garde operation. As a rule, novelties have always attracted me,
and once I find myself in the hands of dentists I have always
tended to consider them, with absolute confidence, as arbi-
trators of my destiny.

'No, no, a dentist can't bear excitement. Let's go ahead
with the treatment, then we'll see.'

When the dentist slipped the probe into the canals, a
paralysing pain ran through me like a flash of lightning, practically nailing me to the ground. I felt chained to the
terrestrial globe from which I had emerged. My jaw fell along
the trajectory of that lightning-bolt, which sought to drag me
to the dark centre of the planet, where Mercury is born with
his liquid metal. Meanwhile, at this time, in the land of myths
and legends, soldiers were running from house to house
arresting citizens of all kinds who then disappeared or were
found dead. The 'colonels' had assumed power, and this made
things even more difficult for me, since I had the almost
impossible task of maintaining contact with our friends in
that nation. The colonels, peacetime bureaucrats, controlled
every movement of every single citizen. These grey men,
dedicated to upholding their own power, made provision for
the introduction of ferocious summary sentences. Afflicted
by toothache, I felt like a ram tormented by a worm digging
tunnels in his brain, forced by the pain to beat his head against
a rock or a tree in the hope either of shaking off the enemy or
of killing himself. The earth, the stone, the world were my life

and my death, from them I drew strength and despair, but I couldn't free myself from them. That tooth, that stranger, that 'other' driven into my body from within, nailed me to the earth.

The pain caused by the probe that slipped into the canals lasted only an instant. Dr Lissauer suddenly withdrew the probe and told me he had done everything he could to save the molar. Finally he succeeded. The abscess disappeared, leaving a little white mark at the centre of the occlusal surface: the filling. I returned to my excursions into the underground passages of the castle, wandering for hours together enveloped in the smell of dust, mildew and rotten wood. From time to time my lover and I would allow ourselves a pause for kisses, embraces, and sometimes more. Agnes was a beautiful brunette with large, immaculate teeth, full lips and a slim figure. That summer our bodies had been seized by a strange ardour. In those unknown cavities of the castle we felt free and innocent, released from everything. Then she married an elderly doctor and I wept for ages, left my job and started working as an assistant in a grocer's shop, unburdening myself with jokes at the expense of the customers. After eight months the filling fell out of its hole and I threw it in the rubbish. For some weeks I didn't have it replaced: I wanted everything in me to rot, nothing mattered to me. When I was struck by a twinge, I decided to go back to Lissauer, who had not the slightest doubt this time.

'You'll have to kill that tooth, but not get rid of it. There's always time for that. So many of us kill ourselves slowly, just by going on living. I'll let you keep the tooth, but I'll fill it with amalgam for you. Then we'll see. It might well accompany you throughout your life, a monument of silver and mercury.'

Over the course of four sessions, the doctor killed the molar, excavated it and then, with a new apparatus, fired in the old miracle cure, the amalgam, that mysterious bond of metals. In the many X-rays carried out over the years, I have always been alarmed to contemplate that tooth, reduced to a very fine covering but solidly planted in my mandible. Inside it was a huge quantity of silver and mercury, from the centre of the earth. At the age of about fifty-five, during a dinner at the German embassy, while munching on a lobster-claw, the vestibular rim of the masticatory surface broke. 'Agnes!' I exclaimed, and everyone looked at me in amazement. I realized that the memory of Agnes, which had so often returned to my thoughts and my dreams, was about to vanish for ever. The pain of the tooth would ease the pain of no longer being able to enjoy the mad and furious love that had filled us back then. The pain was actually supplanted by tremendous twinges which were due to an inevitable bacterial infiltration and the abscess that followed on from it. The tooth had to be extracted to avoid the persistence of a dangerous breeding-ground of micro-organisms – what is called a granuloma. I can't remember who carried out the extraction, which was terribly painful, but I remember perfectly the hand that pulled my head upwards, my desire to try to rise up and help that force, and the sad feeling of being shamefully anchored to the earth, in whose belly I had my roots.

In New Delhi, Dr Sauerwein offered to install a new molar and, since I was to be spending a few months there as a financial consultant to the Indian film industry, this time, with

belated enthusiasm, I accepted the experiment. Hammering
for over two hours, the young Erwin Sauerwein, the son of
the more expert and renowned Egon, who was by then
ninety years old, installed the titanium implant, on to which
he then screwed the artificial tooth.

Less than two years had passed when my bone expelled the
implant and, along with it, the false tooth. At the same time
vanished the memory of the hammering with which
Sauerwein had tried to nail me to my fleeing life, to myself –
which I was fleeing even more feverishly – and with it vanished my pain. With all my being I wanted to rejoin that
'other' of which I merely had an intuitive sense, like a vague
presence in the unfathomable depths of the universe. Vanished
were those metaphysical memories, and back came the
memory of Agnes, the girl with whom I had wandered so
long in the belly of the earth. I recalled, as a painfully remote
sensation, the ardour of our bodies. 'How could all that have
been? Was I the boy that I see with the eyes of memory? My
imagination can't identify with him. None of that ever
existed,' I said to myself the day the false LR6 fell out. 'I have
never existed. I am the memory of a memory of a memory.'

UR6

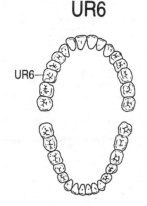

UR6

At the age of forty-two, when I knew that I was going to be spending some time first in Spain and then in Italy, I was advised to study the basic principles of the Catholic religion so that I might more easily understand the minds of the people among whom I would be living. I subjected myself to a lengthy preparation with the help of a priest who was particularly well versed in theological questions, but who also treated the atheist regime in which I lived with a certain tolerance. Abysses opened up ahead of me, and from them rose the peaks of a civilization of which I knew very little, but which, in my eyes, possessed an enormous power of suggestion.

'Don't make the mistake of the neophyte,' the old priest warned me. 'Set enthusiasm aside. Faith needs constancy more than fervour. You are neither St Paul nor St Francis: so you are better off thinking like an employee.'

'You're talking to me as if I were someone to be converted.'

'That's my duty as a man of the cloth. I know you think of me as an instrument and that's that. And I am one, but in much more powerful hands than yours. Cheer up, though, you're about to be interrogated. I'm going to be worse than an inquisitor, even if you're the one who could send me to the pyre.' He gave me a full and proper examination, after which I never saw him again. He was probably arrested, or perhaps killed by some incurable illness.

Just as I was leaving for the Iberian peninsula in my capacity as an expert in cultural exchanges, I remembered that priest. I had been literally subjugated by everything that civilization had produced over two thousand years in the field of the visual arts and music, by its vast spiritual possibilities. It was as though my senses had been roused from a long sleep, sometimes with disastrous effects (see p. 211 ff.). Then I sought to impose upon myself the calm of mediocrity. In this I succeeded effortlessly.

One day I decided to go for a dental check-up. In the Barcelona phone book I found the number of a certain Dr Carlos Kraus, so I went to see him. Thus, by pure chance, began a challenge which would last for twenty years.

The previous day, I had stopped to look at the Church of the Sagrada Familia – in all its reckless upward soaring and intimidating incompleteness. I immediately found myself comparing it to the mind and body of man. Throughout my visit to the dentist I could think of nothing else. The more he disparaged the state of my teeth, the more I brooded on the reason for such negligence: the great and irrepressible disquiet that I constantly felt in my soul.

'Your teeth are in a pitiful state. Not to mention your gums. Why have you neglected them like this?'

'Actually I haven't neglected them. I go to the dentist fairly regularly. It's just my destiny.'

'It isn't destiny. Three of your teeth don't have so much as a scratch, and the gums surrounding them are in good condition as well.'

'It must be coincidence.'

'I don't think so,' said the doctor with a smile. He was a man of about fifty, bald, with black whiskers and a paunch. 'I don't believe in coincidence. Those three teeth,' he indicated UR6, LL6 and LR4, 'in my view represent . . . three religions. The three monotheist religions.'

'You really think so?'

'Yes. I'm convinced of it. We could try an experiment. Let's assign a religion to each of the three teeth. The tooth that lasts longest is the true faith. The other two are the ones that aren't authentic. You remember the story of the three rings, in Boccaccio's *Decameron*?'

'Yes, but you're saying the opposite of Boccaccio. As far as I can see you and my three teeth are deciding which is the true faith, while the *Decameron* speaks of a parity between the Hebrew, Christian and Muslim religions.'

'Let's make a bet,' said the dentist with a mad gleam in his eye. 'Let's abandon the three teeth to their fate. If you promise me to convert to the religion whose representation survives the longest in your mouth, I undertake, with a notary's letter, to leave you half of my possessions. You can see that I'm fairly rich, can't you?'

I was flabbergasted. The dentist stuffed a cylinder of cotton wool, of the brand called Luna 2000, into my mouth to absorb my salivation.

'Think on it, while I do a little clean and check that there aren't any hidden caries. At the end of the session you can tell me whether you accept or not.'

'What if the tooth that lives longest is the one that . . .'

Inserting the mirror into my mouth, he stopped me from continuing.

'If the most vital tooth is the one representing the religion to which you were born, you will have won again. But in the other two cases, without a public conversion I won't leave you a penny.'

The dentist was trying to provoke me. He clearly didn't believe in human rectitude and fidelity. I knew how to respond to such a provocation by a genuine Christian Shylock. (Or was the doctor of Shylock's faith, and was he putting me to the test? Or, final hypothesis, was he a follower of Muhammad wanting to convert me?) However, he issued his challenge again.

'Fine, I accept the bet,' I moaned. 'But I'd like to know the exact sum that's at stake.'

'The notary,' answered the dentist. 'You will find out every-thing from the notary. If your winnings don't seem high enough, if the price of conversion is not to your satisfaction, you will have the chance of pulling out.'

In his madness, however, the dentist wanted to humiliate

me: even to bargain over the money would have been a sign of abject betrayal on my part. I accepted this clause, convinced as I was that the dentist would finally admit that it was a joke or an innocuous provocation.

But Dr Kraus insisted. 'Do you want us to arrange a meeting with the notary for tomorrow?' he asked, proceeding to carry out a summary polish of the teeth using Harvey's rotating disc.

I was appalled. I took my arm out from beneath the paper towel, shook his hand, looked him in the eye and said, very seriously: 'But do you have children?' The man's big black eyes fixed sadly on mine, as if their gaze wanted to enter my head. They shone with a very intense, black light.

'I have no children,' answered Dr Kraus. 'I have many relatives, but I don't want to leave them anything. What have they done for me? Nothing. The other day, as you know, there was a serious attack in Madrid, and a man is dead. I would have liked to have been in his place, I envy him his death. You jump in the air, there's a moment of pain and then you explode into a thousand pieces. It's an end that you might wish for anyone. However, I'm not mad, I just like games of chance. I go to the casino every week. I always win, how boring it is. Well, this is a good game, a game of great ideals, issues more elevated than the human mind can conceive of. And not only the mind: the heart, the soul as well.'

I would have liked to ask Maestro G. for help, but I didn't know where he was at that moment, and anyway betting was not part of his mentality, his concept of the world.

'To judge from the excellent state of the three teeth, before the final verdict we have fifteen or perhaps twenty years ahead

of us. You might die, I might die. You're not risking much.
Go on, accept,' whispered Dr Kraus.

I couldn't decide, I was afraid of a trap, but on whose part?
Simple, pure chance, the nobility of a bet born of the
moment, was something inconceivable to me, given my
obsessive suspicion about everyone and everything.

'The chief condition, obviously, is that no one will touch
the three teeth. You mustn't go to a dentist without my
knowing. If one of the three teeth should give you pain, you
must tell me. This is, it seems to me, a fundamental clause.
Otherwise I grant you complete freedom to treat the teeth
adjacent to those three, and that is a considerable concession,
given that the position, inclination and stability of the chosen
teeth depends on them.'

I didn't reply. I accepted the challenge out of inertia, unable
to resist his offer. That evening I told Rachel everything. At
first she was furious. 'How could you leave your faith to
chance?' she cried. During the night we tossed and turned in
bed. Suddenly, Rachel whispered to me: 'Look at the joke
fate is playing on us. We could get rich. The tooth representing our religion will have to break. What do you think?'

'Break UR6?' I asked.

'That's right. I could take care of it myself,' Rachel continued in a whisper.

'You want to knock out one of my molars,' I thought.
'With one punch you could avenge yourself for all the betrayals, all the wrongs you've endured. I won't give you that
satisfaction.'

Towards dawn, I began to find Rachel's plan rather more
appealing: freeing myself from UR6 and then, in some way, of

one of the other two, making a small renunciation of my faith
and pocketing the money promised by the dentist. But was I
sure of his boasts? Was he really so rich? I decided to make
some enquiries, since I was not short of acquaintances who
might be useful in this. Thus I discovered his history.

His son, a dentist like himself, had transferred at the age of
twenty-five from Barcelona to Vienna, the family's city of
origin. He left home one morning, and from that day there
was no further trace of him. His father hired private detectives
and even clairvoyants, but with no result. His forty-five-year-
old wife, in a fit of cynicism, had run off with a petty thief,
taking money, silverware, jewels. The dentist really had nothing to lose. He was devoted to all kinds of games of chance,
and twice a week he took part in spiritualist sessions in an
attempt to make contact with his son, whom he now imagined to be in the hereafter.

'I will never take advantage of the desperation of a man like
that,' I said to Rachel once I had that information.

'You're right,' Rachel said, 'you're right. But I'm sure you
won't stop thinking about that stupid bet. So you might as
well accept.'

I took her advice, we went to the notary, and the waiting
began. After a year, I found myself in the surgery of Dr Kraus:
an enormous caries had opened up in UR6. 'Yes, it's a nasty
bit of decay, one that might seriously compromise the tooth's
survival. But I give you my word as a gentleman that I will do
everything I can to save it. And you won't have to pay a
thing. I know you're attached to your religion, you're not a
sceptic, that stupid abattoir means something to you. Even if
it takes me ten sessions, I'll save that tooth.'

'But I have to get back to my own country,' I stammered.
'I'm leaving in ten days' time.'

'In ten days I'll have it cured,' said Dr Kraus.

He was a terrific dentist, perhaps the best in the whole of
Catalonia. He used the most secure polymers, and for the
occlusal surface of the Black's cavity he employed a liquid
that he had had brought in from the United States. He also
performed a general clean.

'You've lost nothing so far. Cheer up, the challenge con-
tinues,' said the dentist, dismissing me. 'Please, pay attention to
your gums. They're still very inflamed. If you're attached to
your teeth, have somebody look at them.'

I returned home. Some days later, Maestro G. arrived as
well. After his splendid concert in the great hall of the
Academy, I told him what had happened. We were reconciled
by now.

'Pay attention,' the Maestro said to me. 'You have saved my
life, now it's my turn. If I know anything about the human
soul, this man has put slow-acting poison in your filling. He
already regrets ever making that stupid bet. Please, make an
appointment to see someone tomorrow.'

The Maestro's suspicions cast me into despair. Was I to rule
out the possibility of making myself rich simply because of a
suspicion? In fact, if I had had the filling of UR6 removed
without the knowledge of Dr Kraus, the bet would no longer
have been valid. I went home in a fury, accusing Rachel of
having led me to the slaughter out of greed.

'But why do you pay any heed to the Maestro's suspicions?
Does he love you more than I do? I feel when you're in
danger, I feel it inside my heart, like anyone who truly loves

someone. I tell you that all these suspicions are pure nonsense. He's the one who wants to hurt you in some way, I can feel it,' she said.

'How dare you slander the only honest person I have known. He's a great artist, he's my spiritual guide. And you just want me to stay in the mud, in the filth of existence.'

Rachel began to cry. 'I've given you two children and you talk to me like that,' she sobbed. That night we slept deeply, as we always did after a dramatic explosion of feelings. Clearly, man is granted sleep to save him from those emotions, but it can often be in league with them.

Next morning I awoke with the anguish of a condemned man. I was frightened for my life. 'Maybe Kraus really has poisoned me. Maybe he's a Secret Service man who's been ordered to eliminate me. I'm done for,' I said to myself, over and over. 'When we become obsessive, it is very easy to pass from one obsession to the next, it's a fate to which many men are prone. I'm a natural candidate for mania.' Throughout the rest of the day I repeatedly weighed up Maestro G.'s alarming warning. 'He wants to deprive me of Dr Kraus's wealth so that he can hold me in his clutches by blackmailing me,' I moaned on to myself. That simple, silly bet was becoming a torment.

After the first stormy stages of that strange experience I gradually calmed down, and given that I was no longer aware, as I had been for the first few days, of the symptoms of every disease, of a fatal attack, I convinced myself that the Maestro had made a mistake. He himself never touched on the subject again. More than ten years passed, during which I forgot the bet. The day foreign troops were pulled out of Afghanistan,

UR6 suddenly began to crumble. I felt the pieces in my mouth, like a shattered bone. For days and days I was spitting out yellowish pieces of tooth. I ran to Dr Taussig, who discovered a complete absence of cement in the tooth.

'Is it my faith that's dissolving?' I wondered. 'Is this what my jaw and my brain are trying to tell me?'

After a few hours of indecision, I phoned Dr Kraus in Barcelona, and announced to him that UR6 might have to be extracted.

'I'm sorry for you. Now you've lost the religion you were born with. Provided you want to go on with the bet?'

'Yes, I'll go on. I want to see what happens in the end,' I answered resolutely.

'So we'll have to meet up again for the final decision. Who knows how much time that's going to take? Let's hope we're both still alive.'

I went to see Dr Taussig, who made me open my mouth wide and took a good long look inside. He announced that UR6 was going to be extracted, but that there was also a more dangerous caries in LR4. I was overjoyed. LR4 is diseased! There's justice in the world! Maybe it will fall out before UR6! LR4 represented, in the terms of my agreement with Dr Kraus, the Catholic religion. The likelihood of my conversion remained remote for the time being. I was beside myself with joy.

Two of the three teeth were now diseased. But would they be the first to fall out? 'Sometimes disease suddenly strikes a healthy subject. Maybe that's how it is with teeth as well,' I thought. I went on waiting.

UR2

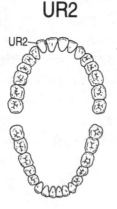

Bruxism

When a human being, for one reason or another, rubs the upper dental arch against the lower for a considerable period of time, exerting pressure from one against the other, he is said to be affected by bruxism. This is an illness which can, without mechanical, psychological or physiological correctives, cause irreversible damage to the lamellar alveolus, the bones of both the mandible and the maxilla, and lead inexorably to the loss of all the teeth.

The causes of bruxism may lie in a state of psychological tension, whether well-founded or not: worry, neurosis (permanent conflict with the reality principle), arterial hypertension, whether hereditary or acquired, intellectual or spiritual ambition, a repressed oneiric tendency and many other things besides. If, one night, hidden microphones were to capture the noise of the teeth of sleeping humanity, we would hear the most unbearable din. While asleep, sixty per cent of human beings grind their teeth against a real or imaginary enemy. This isn't the innocuous practice of gritting one's teeth to confront adversity, to spur oneself on to achieve a task (although even then we might wonder what the violence of the gesture might mean). The things that are being abraded are the most terrible weapons that nature has placed at our disposal, to enable us to tear to pieces, to dismember a potential source of food, an aggressor or something that we wish to attack. To judge from our reactions when punching, kicking, gripping, the bite of the teeth gives us the means to become murderers.

After Maestro G. had made his attempt on my life (see p. 145), for a good five years I was affected by a form of bruxism. At first, Rachel woke me every night by nudging me vigorously in the ribs: 'Stop grinding your teeth,' she whispered to me. 'You've been making that noise for three hours, you won't let me sleep.' Sometimes she asked me questions of universal import: 'What's wrong with you? Is it remorse for the bad things you've done? Has some evil spirit entered you, is it now tormenting you?' she asked, having woken me by shaking me by the shoulders. 'Is it here again? Chase it away!' she murmured in a heartfelt way on other occasions. After three months of these forced awakenings, one night Rachel gave me a slap and I, as a reflex, gave her a kick in the shins. Then I switched on the light and opened my eyes. She was sitting on the bed. She was weeping silently. 'You've got to get yourself treated. If you keep on grinding your teeth like that I'm going. I don't want to sleep on the floor, we're not going to get a bigger house, so there's nothing for it but to go back to my parents. I can't bear to see you like this.'

'Does it bother you so much that I grind my teeth? It's barely audible,' I whispered with all the humility of which my false consciousness was capable.

'It's not that. You're hiding something from me. There's something monstrous within you.'

'There's something monstrous stirring in all living creatures.'

'In all living creatures there's something good as well. I've only seen the monstrous thing in you for some time now. What's wrong with you?'

Without even knowing why, I started talking about the Maestro. 'He scares me,' I said. 'Every time I meet him I fall into despair. He just stands there silently, looking almost half-witted. I wonder what's going through his mind. I just see an empty, vague man looking ahead of him, or, in restaurants, chewing, looking at the landscape. It makes me feel over-whelmed by the futility of life. And yet sometimes he can come out with some intelligent things, phrases that open up abysses. I could kill him. Being suspended between great heights and unfathomable depths like that makes me terribly angry. I could kill him.'

'And that's why you grind your teeth?'

I realized the absurdity of my self-defence. This time, before I confronted the dentist, I went back to Professor Ivan, a psychiatrist of some renown. He measured my arterial pressure, examined the backs of my eyes, asked me if I could remember what day of the week and what year it was, made me do some sit-ups, stretch my arms in front of me with my eyes closed, asked me about my work and my private life and prescribed me a mild tranquillizer.

'Read long, tranquil novels like *War and Peace* or *Joseph and his Brothers*, keep your mind occupied and take a few weeks' holiday.'

'But I can't take holidays whenever I feel like it.'

'Yes, I can see that might be difficult.'

In passing, I also mentioned the Maestro. Professor Ivan took a long look at me. Then he declared that there are strange people in the world.

'But the person in question isn't strange,' I said. 'It's just this that's strange.'

Professor Ivan shrugged his shoulders. 'Artists,' he said, and dismissed me.

The bruxism didn't go away, and my dental arch continued to suffer as a result. Because of this disagreeable phenomenon, each day my teeth became a little shorter.

In the end, I had to yield to Rachel's injunction and went to see Dr Lubetzki, telling him about the case. I revealed nothing about the elusive character of my famous friend, my continuing suspicion that I had invested my emotional energies in a genuine nobody. In any case, as one famous writer puts it, even the greatest genius is no more than meaningless froth on the waves of time and history. Clearly, this observation could not be the true cause of my bruxism. A great sense of worry had begun to gnaw away at me, after I had received that punch from the Maestro. An animal, a nocturnal monster had come to dwell in me: misery.

Dr Lubetzki advised me to put in my mouth a little apparatus that he had had made for himself in a dental technician's laboratory – the Wendell-Mazursky appliance.

'This machine will prevent you from closing your mouth when you are asleep. But if you have the patience to wear it in the daytime as well, you will derive enormous benefit from it. If, on the other hand, you are negligent, your teeth will soon fall out. They will shorten, they will wobble; the periodontitis is to some extent due to occlusion, that is, it is the result of an imperfect closure of the teeth.'

The little apparatus was ready within a few days: it was a kind of false palate, held in place at the sides by a steel structure. Effectively, applying it to the upper arch, I was not able to close my mouth completely. When I said goodnight to Rachel, the voice of a half-wit emerged. During those months, my virility, already unsteady, completely abandoned me.

One morning some time later, crossing the Chain Bridge, I threw the little appliance into the river. When I returned home, I started to look for it and accused first my wife and then the children of having carelessly thrown it out with the rubbish. I made a terrible racket, and the neighbours turned up. Rachel stopped waking me because of the unpleasant bruxism. The periodontitis, on the other hand, advanced inexorably, and maybe that, in some unmentionable way, is what I wanted. The bruxism ceased with the extraction of UR2, the second upper right incisor, which had fallen out for reasons of its own. It was one of my finest and most representative teeth, the pride of my smile. Once I stopped smiling, I also stopped 'bruxing' – my face had become a marble mask.

LR5

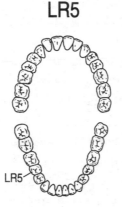

LR5

A tangential story

My lower right second premolar is laterally placed. It hides beneath the inner surface of the gum. With this tooth goes a tangential story.

Dr Lissauer told it to me while he was busy filling, with amalgam, LR5. I kept that filling for exactly forty-five years. The filling was carried out on the eighth of August, the same day, forty-five years later, that the premolar relinquished its place in my lower jaw. It was no longer in a state of decay, but it had to be extracted to make room for my dentures. I remember the day the filling was done, just as I remember the one on which LR5 was extracted. During the afternoon of that first day, foreign troops crossed the borders of an Asian country; in the course of the second, foreign troops crossed the borders of a country that was then called Armenia. On the first occasion, there gradually emerged from the void the face of an old lady with extraordinarily fine and regular features, a face I had never seen before; on the second, that same face reappeared. During those forty-five years, the story that goes with that face had lain hidden in some cell in the posterolateral area of my cerebral cortex, my memory, locating it close to LR5.

The day of the filling of a small caries and the preparation of the Black's Class II cavity in that tooth, I saw a very beautiful old lady coming out of Dr Lissauer's surgery, and when my turn came I asked the dentist about her. Without the slightest misgiving he told me the little old lady's tale of adventure. I will sum it up as best I can. Lissauer took two hours to tell it, but he was very verbose and his digressions often took him far from the point of the matter, which was more or less as follows.

Sara Weiss was the only daughter of a rich shoe salesman, who had arrived in my city from Poland. She was very beautiful. Her parents had brought her up in luxury. She had learned four languages, she played the piano, went to the most elegant resorts, skied with absolute assurance. At a ball at the age of twenty she met a type of swindler, a gambler and cardsharp, fell in love with him and gave herself to him. When the shoe merchant Erwino Weiss found out about this, he called his daughter to him and ordered her to sever relations with that unsuitable character. As for her, she would be sent to France, to college, and he would never allow her to return to her own country. Sara replied that she was a slave to love, and that she could never part from the man.

'Then let me tell you that as far as I am concerned you are
dead,' her father said through his tears. He gave her a little
money, and despite the pleading of his wife he sent her away.
He observed the eight days of mourning sitting on the floor,
shoeless, with his clothes ripped to shreds. His relations came
to bring him food and wept with him over the 'death' of his
daughter. After a few months, Sara was abandoned by the
man who had seduced her, and suddenly she found herself on
the streets. Despite her great beauty and the refinement of her
education, the girl ended up in a brothel on Conti Street, in
the dark heart of the Eighth District. For some years she had
to satisfy minor officials, artisans, porters, pickpockets. One
day a man came to her who treated her with respect and rev-
erence: he was the barber that Sara's father used. The barber
told Erwino Weiss what he had seen, but the old man
answered him: 'I don't know what you're talking about, God
took my poor daughter from me a long time ago, peace to her
soul. And anyway I'm amazed that you go to such places.'

A week later, the shoe salesman closed his shop on People's
Theatre Street and in two months had died of a broken heart.
The barber went to the brothel on Conti Street and respect-
fully asked for the hand of Miss Sara Weiss. He paid the price
requested, married her and they had two lovely children.
They enjoyed twenty years of well-being and tranquillity
together. The barber always regarded that most beautiful lady
as the purest flower of the district. She took care of the house
and the children, and in the evening, for an hour or so, she
played popular songs on the piano, as well as Bach preludes
and Beethoven sonatas. For her unconditional love, and also
for her acceptance of the basest and most brutal form of love,

she had been rewarded with love of a different kind, untempestuous and unemotional. Which of those three was real love?

Then, once again, fate took everything from Sara. Why? There are no answers. The war began, her two sons were called up and died in the ice of the Russian wastes, her husband was killed by a stray bullet during the final days of that terrible slaughter. The former daughter of good family, then a prostitute of the lowest kind and thereafter mother of an exemplary family, she once more found herself alone and without any apparent reason to go on living. At the end of the war, on a day in May, Sara saw an old man of distinguished appearance among the black marketeers. He helped her to buy some eggs and a kilo of flour, she went home with him, and in the weeks that followed she attended to all his needs. This man was a famous musician, who first took her into his home as a housekeeper and then married her. It was towards the end of this complicated life that Sara began to go to Dr Lissauer's surgery to have her teeth treated. Lissauer had also been her father's dentist.

Over the years I have learned that there is no such thing as a tangential story: either all stories are tangential, or none of them are. They all touch each other, cross paths in some way or another. There is no escaping this, even if it seems that life becomes fragmented into a series of rapidly changing images with no apparent connection, links will unexpectedly be revealed.

From the less than well-meaning stories of my mother's sisters, I learned one day that my father used to frequent Sara Weiss at the time when she was in the brothel on Conti

Street, and possibly afterwards as well. They even spoke, somewhat sarcastically, of a 'great love' between the two of them. What? Is there a fourth kind of love apart from the self-less, the base and the tempestuous kinds? Yes, there are loves without purpose or substance, which drag on for decades. I am not even condemning them. They are like tangential stories: they can suddenly descend upon us, inspiring us or showing us the futility of our certainties.

I have kept LR5 in a metal container. Sometimes I take it out of my box of junk and look at it, and all of a sudden I see the face of Sara Weiss, the elegant little old lady with the alert and unfathomable expression. Her face exists in my memory now as she died many years ago.

GUMS

I met Professor Essender in Wolfsburg, where I was afflicted by a terrible attack of gingivitis. I had gone to that town in northern Germany to deliver a lecture on the philosophy of the motor car. This little dissertation had enjoyed a certain popularity, particularly in those countries which were, for a time, known as eastern, thanks to its original attitude towards the car. My idea was extremely simple, and I defend it to this day. The motor car is, even more than a phallic symbol and an instrument of aggression, the representation of the mother's womb. I am not the first to put forward this hypothesis, but I alone have dedicated one hundred and fifty pages to it. Amongst other things, the sensation of well-being that I have experienced when driving or being driven in a car is perhaps one of the most reassuring pleasures of life. I have been driven, fast asleep, for hundreds of kilometres, and I have slept soundly while my relations, in mourning, accompanied me to the funerals of my father and my uncles. For many years, like so many parents of our time, in order to send Leah and Gerson to sleep I used to put them in the car at nine in the evening, consigning them once more to Rachel's maternal arms, serenely slumbering, at half-past nine.

In Wolfsburg I briefly summed up the chapters of my essay, read two passages out loud and received the praise of the directors of a large car factory and the applause of the audience. After a generous dinner in an Italian restaurant, I returned to my hotel and prepared to go to bed. Brushing my teeth with the disinfecting brush I had found in the bathroom, I felt a pain in my gums that was completely new to me, accompanied by an unprecedented haemorrhage. To tell the truth, every time I felt weak and an inflammation was at work in some part of my body, my gums swelled up and began to bleed. I had learned everything about this condition from my earlier experiences, but during this rather agitated period of my life I had neglected the routines of oral hygiene, concentrating as I was on making a career and winning the love of the various women I encountered (it was never enough for me, especially since, because of my blind floundering in the ocean of femininity, I had by then received more slaps and insults than kisses and caresses. And this holds true, or even more so, for my wife, who was faithful unto death).

A visit was scheduled, for the morning after the lecture, to the car factory that employed almost all the inhabitants of the town. Worried by the haemorrhage, I mentioned it to the organizer of the conference. 'You're in luck. Don't you know that we have one of the world's great specialists here? I'll call him right now, he'll be happy to see you. He loves literature and essay-writing. I'm sure he'll see you this very evening,' said my kind protector. At three o'clock in the afternoon I was in the little villa of Professor Essender (his name literally translated means 'Eating'), and sat down in a waiting room furnished with black leather armchairs probably inherited from the professor's grandfather and preserved by the latter with genuine love.

Above them, on the walls, paintings of uncertain era but undoubted value exhibited their own antiquity. During the hour of waiting, smiling nurses crossed the room, calling loudly to the patients whom they greeted with familiarity. So I too was about to enter Professor Essender's 'family', I too was about to enjoy the benefits of his brilliant invention. This consisted in taking from the gums a microscopic piece of tissue to put it in a culture like a bacillus. After thirty or forty days of treatment with nutritional materials, the few cells would multiply, and within six months the professor would have a piece of tissue the size of a steak. Grafting the artificially produced gums back into the patient's mouth was a relatively simple procedure. The new tissue would cover the terminal parts of the teeth, as if the gums had never decayed.

But there was one drawback to this ingenious procedure; since the bone that was supposed to support that artificial flesh could not be regenerated, the gums tended to recede after a short time, and they never provided the stability necessary for teeth that were already a little mobile, shaky, relinquished by the grip of the body that wished to expel them like undesirable aliens. (I have always thought that periodontitis is one of the most obvious signs of the rejection of one's neighbour, or more generally of the 'other', and thus also of the world and of God. My meeting with Professor Essender convinced me of the opposite.)

After about an hour's wait, a charming nurse came to call me to take me into the professor's consulting room. In other little rooms, young doctors and nurses were carrying out simpler operations of restoration and prevention. Professor Essender, of medium height, with a jovially broad face and sparse, thin white hair, greeted me, indicated for me to sit in the usual dentist's chair and asked me what my problem was.

'I'm afraid when I open my mouth you'll see for yourself: my teeth and my gums present a tragic picture,' I said.

'Let's not exaggerate. Open your mouth for a moment.'

I did so with a sense of inescapable shame and guilt I could never describe. Professor Essender barely glanced at them, then he announced: 'I've seen worse, much worse.'

'Unfortunately I can't treat my teeth as I should like to, my job, the life I lead, won't let me,' I answered.

'What do you do?' the professor asked a little distractedly. I didn't know how to reply, so I stammered out a few phrases, told him of my numerous jobs, my constant travels.

'I never manage to stay in the same place for more than two weeks. There's no point in my trying to explain my erratic life, I'm sure you'll be able to discern it for yourself, any phenomenon can be better observed from without than from within. Evasion, pursuit, rejection and metaphysical affirmation of identity, etcetera.'

Professor Essender brightened up. 'Then perhaps you know what my profession is?' he asked.

It was a strange, somewhat rhetorical question, coming from the mouth of one of the most famous specialists in the world. 'Now I consider myself,' he continued solemnly after a brief pause, 'more a student of art history than a dentist. I am about to publish a book on Goya. I think that few people know his paintings as well as I do. And I possess eight paintings by that great genius. By cultivating the flesh of my clients I have earned enough to be able to dedicate myself to the spirit.'

The professor spoke to me at length of the great Spanish painter, of the Roman period that he had discovered by chance, through his tireless investigations. He talked for about half an hour with dilettante enthusiasm and the competence of a trained academic. Of the old master's years in Bordeaux, and of his terrible loneliness, he gave a moved and moving account. 'We all end up like that. Those fantasies torment us, kill us. We are victims of our minds, my dear sir. The myth of the mind is the worst of man's inventions,' he concluded.

Having planted this time-bomb in my brain, the professor fell silent for several seconds, then abruptly changed his tone. 'Open your mouth,' he whispered, absorbed. He felt my teeth with his fingers, tapping them with the handle of the Lecleuze lever. 'You'll take them to the grave,' he said, with great conviction.

I was transfixed by these words, which were like those uttered by my mother many years previously (see p. 23). Either she or the dentist had a clear image of me as a corpse. But the professor's words contained an ulterior motive.

'You mean that I'm only going to live another few years, that my teeth won't have time to fall out because I'll die first? Or are you prognosticating a long life, and seeing in my teeth the same clumsy tenacity that has always accompanied my character?' I silently asked myself.

It was when LR5 came out that I was freed from the nightmare of that ambiguous verdict. 'You see, Professor Essender was mistaken, I will survive my teeth, those strangers who have come to dwell in me, that have crystallized in me, like Lot's wife at the sight of Sodom and Gomorrah in flames.'

A few months later I had a flash of inspiration. The removal of a piece of gum and the regrafting of the new tissue transformed me into a genuine monster. The injection of osteoblasts into my flesh, the formation of a bony support bathed by the blood that poured over it, not passing through my capillaries but, as in the cavernous body of pain, simply filling the porosity of the bone, made a bleeding mask of me for several weeks. My face swelled up with purple haematomas, I couldn't eat, even breathing caused me great effort and intense pain.

One day, while I was lying like that in my little hospital bed, Professor Essender came to find me, made me get up and led me into his private gallery where the Goya paintings were kept. With much ceremony he threw open the doors and introduced me into his sanctuary. The grace of those luminous paintings did not ease the pain of my swollen face, and I stood there like Quasimodo facing Esmeralda, while Professor Essender whispered to me, his breathing laboured: 'Have you ever seen anything more beautiful? Wouldn't you give all your teeth, and even an arm or a leg, for just one of these masterpieces? Anyway, what are teeth for? To show aggression to things and people. Meanwhile you could stand in front of these paintings lost in admiration, disarmed and moved, for your whole life.'

In a flash I understood the meaning of my illness. Thanks to it, that is, thanks to the weakness of my gums, and thanks to the presence of bacteroides gingivales and actinobacillus, in old age I would be ready to set aside my defences, saying to life and death: 'Come and get me, I'm not putting up any resistance.' And no one, not even my worst enemy, would make me grind my teeth, all of which had by now fallen out. Instead I would reveal my mouth wide open, the dark cavern of my defenceless nothingness.

UL3

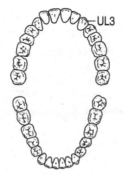

Vampire teeth

UL3 is the vampire canine. It began to lengthen, to attain its definitive dimensions, around my forty-fifth year.

One evening, when I got home, I found Rachel in tears. 'Blood,' she said. 'Blood. It's come.' She smiled radiantly and cried. I couldn't understand her joyful despair. The next morning she took me by the hand and led me into the cellar. At one spot in the moist and mildewed ground of the narrow corridor there was a little fresh pile of clods of earth. 'We've buried it here.'

'What?' I asked.

'Leah was absolutely terrified. She wanted to bury her linen here with the traces of her first blood.'

It was cold in the cellar, and as I breathed I felt a twinge in my upper left canine. My gums had receded and the neck thus uncovered had grown sensitive. I was turning into a vampire. I smiled at the idea, since I had only hitherto felt 'good' emotions towards my daughter, and she had probably felt the same about me. Nothing had ever given me greater serenity than my rare conversations with Leah, in the kitchen, outside on Sunday walks, travelling in cars. With me Leah was smiling, loving, fierce. Her face was perfectly regular: almond eyes, straight little nose, harmonious lips, pleasant chin with a little cleft in the middle. She had only one defect: her upper left canine was too large in comparison with her other teeth. We started to address the problem quite late, when Leah was already thirteen. Dr Hönig, whom we took her to see, declared us the guilty parties, and said that the little one would have to bear for ever the consequences of our negligence. Without drastic intervention, the canine could not be reduced to the scale of her other teeth. For a long time I imagined that, throwing herself at my neck, Leah might one day or other suck my blood, as my old age was now inadvertently doing to her youthful vitality. But too many novels have already been written on this eternal and reciprocal vampirism between the younger and older generations, there's no point dwelling on it again. Between Leah's first blood and Rachel's last, my teeth fell out one by one. Unrelenting desire and silent music sustain the miserable deception, the mask of my being.

LR4

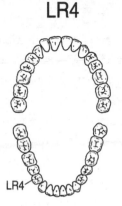

LR4

An error of faith

This is the second stopping-point among my three sound teeth.

Five years after my meeting with Dr Kraus, LR4, the lower right first premolar, whose good health I had discovered only at the age of forty-two (the age of a great return to faith), was covered, suddenly, with a greenish tartar. LR4 was associated in my mind with the Catholic religion. That tartar was the first sign of corruption, and Dr Schwartz decided to scratch it away with his terrible Darby-Perry scraper, and the even more terrible one invented by Dr E. Younger. In all likelihood that corruption had a non-causal relationship with a new attitude in my response to this religion, and the build-up of detritus

formed the prelude to a 'polish' that might signify the desire
for clarification, for the elimination of bad things, as well as
the proliferation of doubts. Five years on Taussig made the
discovery of the first caries. What had happened? Something
that I had thought would never happen to me until the end of
my days. I was about to decide the question of the true faith
without the verdict of my teeth. Once again I was influenced
by a tangential story, in this case one with notable force. Here
is a short account of that experience.

A distant relation of mine, with whom I shared a bench at
school, went to live in Palestine some months after the end of
the war. For a short time, David had shown himself, in the
games played between the closed stalls of the neighbouring
market, to have a genuine talent for football, which is why his
decision to abandon a potentially brilliant career seemed all
the more rash. A year after he left, David suddenly reappeared
among us as though nothing had happened. But during that
year his former ability had vanished and he never wanted to
play football again. He lived alone with his mother on the
ground floor of an old two-storey house on Republic Square.
She was a thin, stooped woman, who worked as a dressmaker
and dressed shabbily. He tried to help her. Then his mother
died and for a while David wasn't seen around. One evening,
some years later, while I was preparing for my leaving exam,
and had gone outside for a breath of air, I met him on the
corner between People's Theatre Street and Adamo Vaj Street.

For a moment he stopped two or three yards away from
me, then he came over and embraced me. We went to the
Circular Boulevard and sat down in a café. Here he told me
how things had been. Never had such bitter words issued

from the mouth of an eighteen-year-old boy. He told me of the hardship of life in the desert among strangers, the unbearable heat and the exhaustion, the illness of his mother, the terrible loneliness of a boy whose entire family, apart from her, had been destroyed. He described to me the difficulty of obtaining permission to return here, the desolation of the journey and what he had found when he got home: dusty memories of people who had ceased to exist. After enumerating all his sufferings, he suddenly told me, with a certain bitter hope, of how in a moment of illumination he had found a new faith, and how a priest had helped him to take the road of conversion to Catholicism. He described to me the hours of catechism, the lessons. 'Until then I had known nothing of what I am learning now,' he said finally. 'Why did fate not have me born to Christian parents?' The question was a thorny one, worthy of a major theological argument, and contained within it the worm of doubt, calling into question, as it did, the perfection of the creation and the theory of original sin which had tarnished it.

Finally, David described to me the ceremony of conversion, the abjuration, the exorcism, the salt on the lips and the oil on the forehead and the contentment of the priest who had reclaimed a soul for salvation. 'Now I live like this, dedicating a good proportion of my thoughts to the mystery of the Holy Trinity, the suffering of Christ crucified, the joy of the Resurrection,' concluded my friend in an artificial tone. For whole days his words rang in my mind and then, gradually, they disappeared into the depths of memory and oblivion.

I practically never saw him again. Fifteen years later, during a dinner of ex-schoolmates, I learned that David had become a priest, and that because of his unshakeable faith he had been persecuted by the regime. Someone said that he was supposed to have been imprisoned and beaten until he completely lost his senses. Another eleven years passed.

On the day of a demonstration ordered by the government against the massacre that had been carried out in the Lebanon, no one knew exactly by whom, but which saw the deaths of hundreds of children and old people deprived of their own land and temporarily housed in two villages, walking up Kun Street I saw a strange-looking Catholic priest. His hair was short, his nose long, his expression filled with lively stupidity. He was advancing with rapid skipping steps, and rubbing his hands. I didn't recognize him but I had a sense that it was he, David Klein. I didn't dare stop him. He went into the chapel of Santa Rita and closed the door. I heard the sound of the bolt. 'It's David,' I thought. 'I'm sure he's joined the demonstration, and he's been shouting against the very people he's descended from!'

This idea impressed me even more than the story of his conversion. For weeks and weeks I turned this story around in my mind. Then it too was covered over and buried.

Another four years went by. It was February and Maestro G., my long-time friend, sent me an invitation to join him in his mountain house in the Dolomites. The tone of the note made it clear that this was work-related. From Rome, where I was currently representing my country's film industry, I took the train and went to meet him. On the first day, the Maestro invited me to a sumptuous dinner in the home of a noblewoman, and got me talking to a Chilean who had lived in Germany for a long time. I felt as if I was sitting an exam.

The second day, we went skiing, and came to a 'black' piste, one that is really quite dangerous. At the opening of a forest of fir trees, a skier came hurtling towards me at terrifying speed and was about to run me down. Throwing myself down into the snow, I was just in time to see him shoot past about a yard away from me. It was him, the Maestro!

He was obviously trying to kill me. I wondered who would have given him the order, but soon my curiosity subsided. That's the question you should never ask. I was left with the great pain of learning that my best friend, whom I had saved from death, was actually prepared to murder me.

We went down the valley and I pretended nothing was wrong, but that same evening I took the train back to Rome. I wrote a letter in which I asked to be recalled to my homeland. I spent some months in fear and despair. Rachel came to get me, but she didn't know how to cheer me up. The friend I most admired was prepared to kill me, that was my only thought during those days. It was an absurd way to think, given my occupation, in which there is no room for emotions of any kind. Yet I still had feelings, and for that reason I planned to abandon my secret work. I wandered the streets of the capital and, going back and forth in time (another thing one should never do), I was gripped by a sense of great discomfort, a great depression, as they called it in those days. Everything struck me as insane, erroneous, vile.

One morning, while I was strolling about near the station, my eye fell on an anonymous and unpretentious-looking church. I don't know why but I went in. I knocked on the grid of the confessional, announced my intention to confess, and on the other side the priest was, of course, delighted. I

don't know how or why it happened, I just know that I
became aware of the need for a long talk with someone.
I talked for an hour in my native tongue. I reviewed my
whole life, the whole sequence of senseless, stupid deeds, all
my dishonesty. I made not the slightest reference to my profession, but more than anything else I lamented the injustice
of being repaid for one's own faith with pain and the threat of
death. I only dared speak of such elevated and mysterious
things because I knew my interlocutor didn't understand me.
He didn't understand me but he said nothing. I was impressed
by his silence. Then he asked me some questions, and in the
end he merely ordered me to say a few Our Fathers, medita-
ting on every word.

'In which language?' I asked.

'In your own,' he said.

'I don't know a word of that prayer in my language,' I
answered.

'Then say it with me, off you go.' He began to recite that
prayer slowly, leaving very long pauses between one phrase
and the next. I thought not about what I was saying, but
about David Klein, seeing in front of me his face as a boy and
then as a childlike old man. For me, faith was contained
within the juxtaposition of those two faces. At some point I
grasped the absurdity of the situation, got up and ran from the
church. For a few days I thought about following my old
classmate's example in one way or another. Then one morning I woke up with terrible toothache. LR4 was decaying, the
pulp was infected.

I phoned Kraus in Barcelona and told him of the disease in
LR4. The Spanish dentist asked for a day to think. Two hours

later he called me back and gave me permission to have the tooth treated by Dr Taussig. I wondered how on earth he knew him, but the day after I went to see Dr Taussig, who performed the filling. He reduced the pulp, prepared a cavity deriving from the contact between an occlusal and a vestibular cavity. This tooth was compromised. But not so much as to have to be extracted or fall out.

After that religious crisis I persuaded myself that this approach to faith, dictated solely by a momentary impulse, was absurd. Was that faith? I had attained wisdom and judgement, but in vain. LR4 remained where it was: patched, internally empty, full of false material, it resisted. But it wasn't the last to leave my mouth. Everything converged to provide instruction of a really superior kind. The patient reader will shortly discover what kind.

LL5

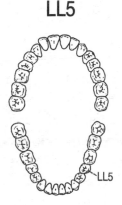

LL5

LL5 was always, for me, an anonymous tooth without any special meaning, until the moment when, at the age of fifty, I unexpectedly discovered its enormous importance. It seemed that that premolar had waited so long in order to reveal itself all at once on a fixed date and time, as happens with fate, attacks, revelations, death. I have already spoken of Maestro G. I spent hours and hours sitting in Dr Taussig's waiting room with him, and he never uttered a word. I never understood who had sent him to this obscure dentist and why. Was it coincidence that he was there? Had he decided to trail me with some particular purpose in mind? We watched each other with a mixture of hatred and affection, not knowing which of the two feelings should prevail. To tell the truth, this artist's character worried me greatly: he had tried to kill me. And yet his appearance, the vacuity of his expression might have made one think the man was a perfect idiot. At the same time the seemingly detestable creature emanated an air of mystery. 'Why don't you get up and return that punch, breaking one of his teeth as he did to you?' I asked myself. 'All artists are nullities as people: they fill up, like flowerpots, with experiences which they then give back to the world in the form of literary, musical, painterly works. They are pots full of dung, as that great mystical text, the *Book of Splendour*, puts it. They are ingrates, murderers.' This is what I thought about him. We studied each other, each waiting for the other to move, to be able to react, to dodge the attack.

After three or four encounters of this kind, the mystery was revealed one day. It was hard to reconcile this scruffily dressed man – his flannel shirts always unbuttoned around neckerchiefs of various colours, his metal-framed glasses with their lenses always steamed up, this caricature of an intellectual – with Maestro G.

Let us return to teeth for a moment. As I have said, LL5 remained in its place for a long time without ever succumbing to disease: it chewed faithfully until, when I reached the age of about forty, its upper equivalent, UL5, was damaged so irrevocably that it had to be extracted by Dr Stadler. Then I stopped chewing with that part of my mouth, and the premolar had nothing further to do, remaining hidden in my cheek and ignored by my tongue, which avoided it as if it didn't exist. For LL5, another ten years passed in complete oblivion. The day of my fiftieth birthday I had the idea of giving myself a present of a local sweet that was sold in very hard blocks, and called 'potato sugar'. I hadn't eaten it for about thirty years. I bought it in a little shop on Friday Street and while I was still paying I nibbled at it. My incisors were not up to penetrating that stone-hard block. So I opened my mouth at the side and attacked the sweet with my molars and premolars. As I bit into it, the pain transmitters flashed a signal to my brain. It was a very strange signal, not a strong one, but one of those that strike one with their breadth: it seemed to me that my whole face was crossed for a moment by a kind of impulse that I could, even today, define only as a flash.

I put the potato sugar in my pocket and left the shop. Immediately, with my tongue and then with the thumb and index finger of my right hand, I began to explore LL5, discovering that my premolar was indeed unsteady in its socket. I was terribly downhearted. I considered the probable and imminent loss of LL5 to be the beginning of senescence and terminal decay. I already envisaged myself as a corpse. I tried, as usual, to cheer up. I went to see Dr Taussig, on People's Theatre Street, for a consultation.

Dr Taussig had recently taken over Dr Lissauer's old surgery and despite the fact that he was over sixty, he hoped to grow rich very quickly, given the lack of oral hygiene in our district and the appetites of its inhabitants. The dentist had studied in Italy and even now, from time to time, he took refresher courses in Padua and Bologna. He had abandoned the major Danubian school of dentistry to dedicate himself to new techniques, most of which were invented in America. The estimate that Dr Taussig gave me for the treatment of my teeth was exorbitant in view of my situation at the time.

It was a matter of fixing a good twelve teeth – all of them more or less decayed – in the upper arch, reducing them to little stumps and covering them with iron and porcelain crowns resembling the original set. The burden of chewing would rest entirely upon these crowns, preserving the jawbone against rupture and the teeth against the danger of falling out. The cost of this long and complicated operation was equivalent to four months' salary for me. It was a procedure that was widely used in other countries, but very little in our own, because of its high cost.

My inner stability, however, depended on these acts of restoration, which I both desired and feared. I was afraid, in fact, that if I took the instrument of such an obvious fiction into my mouth, I would always feel myself to be a kind of simulacrum, a ghost, a living corpse. On the other hand, the idea that I might shortly become a toothless old man terrified me: I was not greatly disposed to give up the joys of life altogether, I didn't yet want to chase the 'she-dog' that stirred inside me. Also, at this time, I had met Livia, whose ancient Roman name heads one of the most restless chapters of my life.

I had no idea how to get hold of all that money. I had been working in television for a short time, and the money I earned was barely enough for my family's needs and my own, as secret as they were indispensable. But I agreed with Dr Taussig on the date on which treatment was to begin, and promised myself that I would live the days that followed in a kind of retreat, from within which I would address my sole true interlocutor, the only one who would be able to help me. The first session was arranged for a Wednesday afternoon.

On Tuesday afternoon my daughter came to see me. With

the directness that I have always adored in her, she told me straight out that the purpose of her visit was to borrow a large sum of money from me. She had been to the dentist, to Dr Hönig, who had discovered that her teeth were in a severe state of decay.

'If you don't make provision for regular treatment, if you don't use ceramic fillings rather than the usual polymers and resins, we'll have to start the whole job all over again in a year, and in two or three years we'll have to take out all your teeth. It's up to you.' My daughter repeated Dr Hönig's words three times, and then got straight to the point.

'My husband is only willing to pay for resin fillings for me. He says he has no money, and he's done the same thing for himself. Either you pay for it, father, or I'll ruin my mouth for ever. Would you like to see me with my mouth completely ruined? Anyway, I can tell you that the porcelain filling costs exactly . . .'

It was the same figure that I was going to have to pay for my own teeth. At this point Leah paused for a long time. The blood rose to my head. I had to choose between my daughter and myself.

Choosing! Why did that horrible task have to be the dominant motif of our lives? Are we allowed to choose whether we come into the world or remain in the limbo of the possible expressions of matter and the spirit? And once we've been hurled into existence, why then must we choose whether to favour someone else, rather than just think of ourselves? Why must we shoulder physical and moral pain so that someone else may be spared it, even if that someone else is our daughter, whom we ourselves have hurled into existence? Fate may take our own daughter and make her an instrument of torture for us!

I sent Leah away without giving her a precise answer. During the night that followed, I insulted that beautiful and lively creature, flinging her back into the void from which she had sprung after a swift embrace with Rachel. Once again, thousands upon thousands of times, I found myself facing the difficult alternative between giving up any semblance of physical vigour once and for all, and assuming a discreetly handsome appearance behind which I might conceal myself, my own fearful and anxious, sly and frightened other self. Thousands upon thousands of times I ran through the vague possibilities of laying my hands on twice the amount of money required, when in reality I didn't even have enough for one of us.

In the middle of the night, animal selfishness began to abandon me, and within me there awoke that higher being who can put a limit on his own good lest he damage the 'other'. In my imagination, my daughter appeared before me toothless, the words came out of her mouth horribly mangled. I imagined her husband's disgust, his reproaches, his words of contempt. My son-in-law, a hydraulic engineer, was not very tolerant of Leah. Her exuberant grace frightened him, making him critical and aggressive. So what was to be done? In my indecision I did that thing that Chekhov describes as the worst tragedy following a disaster: I went to sleep. I dreamed of Judith and Holofernes; a solemnly festive air surrounded the two figures as though there was no enmity between them, as though everything was bound to converge peacefully on the perfect fulfilment of the rite. 'I,' I thought in my dream, 'am of course Holofernes, even if I don't identify with him, and my daughter is Judith. What are we going to do? Will she kill me? Or is it better for me to kill her, seeing as I know how this story ends?'

I awoke in good humour; that dream, so calm and, as I have said, so solemn, prompted my decision. I telephoned Dr Taussig to ask him for an appointment. I wanted him to extract LL5 that same day, so that I wouldn't have to think about it any more. I didn't know how I would find the money for my daughter, but by now I was no longer worried about that – the choice between her and me, between me and whoever else, was made.

Then I went to the office, where I met Livia (see the chapter entitled 'Galvanic pain'). Everything was called into question once again. In the afternoon I went back to Dr Taussig's surgery to embark upon a new discussion and try to find some way out. I had no wish to appear like a man about to enter old age before the woman I had fallen in love with the very moment I saw her. There, in the waiting room of the dental surgery, was Maestro G. For the first time in years we addressed each other. Two men who had tried to kill one another talked peaceably about dental treatment and money. After half an hour he offered me the money required for both treatments. Was it perhaps an attempt to enrol me in the ranks of another secret service? The issue is too complicated to be told solely as part of the story of LL5: I will discuss it in relation to three other teeth. Let this suffice: in the end I abandoned the expensive porcelain apparatus, LL5 grew mobile in its socket, and two years later it became infected. But at this point I gave thanks to fate, since I preferred to face up to old age rather than enter a fresh emotional storm. LL5 was the sign of disorder and chaos, as I would understand only many years later.

That evening, I jotted down the following in my dental diary: 'The wise men of the school of Babylon were right when they concluded that the creation of man was not a blessing.'

LL3

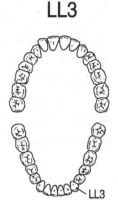

LL3

I tried to sever the thread of pain on Yom Kippur in the year five thousand seven hundred . . . I was in Hyderabad, on a secret mission, with a consignment of arms. Officially, I was organizing an exhibition of drawings by the Hungarian artist Grosz, within the ambit of cultural exchanges between my country and Pakistan.

During those days in Hyderabad, the only European with whom I managed to exchange four words at the sailing club was Dr Hirsch. The dentist's wife was a buxom English blonde, clearly ripe for any erotic adventures. Two days before the Day of Repentance, the dentist invited me into his surgery. At the time I wasn't going to the dentist's very regularly, and was quietly letting my teeth turn yellow. The dentist wanted to test out laughing gas on me – it was still in use in those days. It was the analgesic he used on his patients. He first tested the gas on a friend, a little pink and smiling man, Mr Jesurum. That wood merchant's face turned even pinker and rounder than before. After having, in her turn, inhaled a good dose of gas, Mrs Hirsch assumed an air of joyful excitement: she took off her shoes and started dancing by herself. I have always been simultaneously very cowardly and very brave. The cowardice derived from my terror in the face of anything new, the courage from the stubborn resignation with which I have given myself up to it.

In the face of laughing gas, I retreated as usual. 'What does this stranger want of me?' I thought. 'Maybe he wants to drug and kill me. Anything could happen here.' I gave the excuse of a terrible headache and went home.

On the eve of the Day of Atonement, I concentrated on the events of my life. Not on those things of which I was guilty – those are things we can never thoroughly know – but on the possibility of dedicating myself from that moment onwards to life and nothing else. At sunset, I evoked within myself images of those members of my family who had died. In my mind's eye I saw a long rank of faces similar to my own, and in spirit I joined them. I asked forgiveness for everything, especially for having come into the world. Suddenly, I felt a pain in LL3.

'What do you want?' I asked the One to whom the pain was connected. No inspiration came, no reply.

'Someone must have created this pain. Does it equate to Evil, and the voice of Evil that speaks within it, or is it rather to do with the One who holds the thread of pain? And if I destroy that pain, does it continue to exist? Or does it exist but remain mute, does it cease to speak to me because its essence is suffering?'

I rebelled at this idea.

Outside in the streets, armoured cars were filing past, ranks of soldiers were leaving for the bloody war that had just begun against a country as poor as their own. The soldiers bellowed, the people shouted and danced in the streets. In that hubbub, my pain seemed to grow even stronger. I was a long way from repentance; I felt a kind of rage within myself. At about four o'clock in the afternoon I called Dr Hirsch, asking him to open the surgery for me. Hirsch listened to me, welcomed me and examined me, announcing in the end that LL3 would stay in place for another five or six years. It would obviously be necessary to check the inflammation and fill the infected canals. Then he put a tube in my mouth, ordering me to take deep inhalations of the gas that would come out of it.

'It's Yom Kippur, I'm sorry to transgress the precepts but, as a good dentist, I am divided between love of man and love of the Eternal One. It is not said that the two shall go hand in hand. Humanity may be repellent, but the matters of the Almighty are often, at least apparently, no less horrible for us.'

He told me to open wide. Feeling like a condemned man, I obeyed. I don't know how much laughing gas I inhaled. The Day of Repentance and Purification passed for me in irrepressible laughter, more blasphemous than a curse. Hirsch, on the other hand, left me alone with his wife, who wanted to run through the whole of her erotic repertoire with me, with such violent urgency that it was almost impossible for me to resist. I was tipsy and excited, and when she undressed and sat on my knees I was filled with an irresistible lust. I felt I was both spectator and actor in a frenetic and disgusting comedy, and I could do nothing in response but laugh, laugh, laugh.

Mrs Hirsch began to involve herself in my life with the same ardour of that afternoon. She turned up at the most inopportune moments, swooping into the countries and cities where I happened to be, so that she could once again enjoy what obsessively flashed through her mind: the exhilarating sweetness of the Day of Purification. I hated her more and more, yet each time I yielded to her very British desires.

One day, Rachel intercepted a letter from her, describing down to the tiniest detail the sequence of events of our first meeting in Hyderabad. Although I marvelled at my erotic imagination, which clearly tended to slumber under normal conditions, my pride soon made way for shame. Rachel, my dear good Rachel, burst into tears, hugged the children, who were already going through adolescence, and asked me a thousand times why I had betrayed her. I could have cited a thousand reasons, all as understandable as they were odious, except that, unlike Kierkegaard, I have always had a horror of the commonplace. That repulsion has often pushed me into play-acting, into cowardly deeds, into fiction. Considering banality a capital sin, I was amazed that it was not considered on a par, for example, with lying. Man is obsessed with truth, and in its name he commits the worst crimes: but how many crimes are committed in the name of everyday banality?

It was after this experience that Rachel and I separated for the first time.

I freed myself from my English girlfriend with some difficulty: I couldn't bear her obsession with savouring over and
over the enjoyment of that first moment, which had made her
shriek with pleasure, as she insisted on trying to rediscover it.
In any case, I was perfectly aware that the word 'love', which
she uttered so often, really represented an irrepressible wish to
make time stand still by means of repetition. That is the meaning of pleasure, and sometimes of laughter. To avoid seeing
Mrs Hirsch again, I resorted to an unusual strategy: I had
LL3, the canine that was the original reason for our meeting,
extracted. The moment I rid myself of that canine essence,
that 'bitch' (as Schopenhauer called sexual desire), greedy Mrs
Hirsch began to love me less, until she disappeared from my
life for ever. For ever! What an expression! In my solitude I
was able to discover that time itself is an obsession. Present,
past, future do not exist: everything is bloody comedy, and the
spirit is like the laughing gas with which Dr Hirsch removed
my taste for repentance at having been born.

LL6 AND UR6

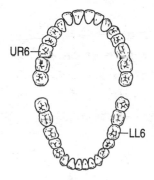

UR6

LL6

LL6 was carious, so Dr Salem had opened up a large cavity in the tooth. It was a Ward's cavity, not a Black's cavity: a hole, in other words, without parallel walls. I found myself in Alexandria and, try as I might, I couldn't find a dentist called Cohen or Grün, or Schwartz or Klein: Dr Salem was an expansive person, always with a ready joke, his eyes liquid and profound. Within that Ward's cavity was sealed everything I had amassed, over the months and years, about the great and mysterious civilization of Islam: from Averroës to algebra, from Firdusi to Omar Khayyam, to anatomy, to hashish, to the *Thousand and One Nights*, to *The Thief of Baghdad*, to the great Mohammed II, the warrior emperor described so well by Babinger.

'Set aside your admiration, please,' the dentist said on the occasion of our conversation preceding the excavation of the tooth. 'We fear those who admire us, and admire those who fear us,' laughed the dentist.

'Our civilization is impenetrable to you. As regards penetration, I have prepared for the caries to be removed from your tooth, but I wouldn't swear that it will be saved for more than . . . let's say three years.' I leapt with joy in the dentist's chair.

'Why are you so pleased?' asked the dentist, puzzled.

I told him the story of the bet. For me, LL6 represented the Islamic religion. He looked at me seriously, told me to open my mouth, examined my teeth again, shook his head.

'I have been a bad Muslim, I should have saved that tooth for good and I haven't managed to do so. For you, on the other hand, it is a great relief. But the final word has not yet been spoken.'

Dr Salem went back to work. He removed the filling he had just put in, and after cementing the root canals to prevent the proliferation of bacteria, he replaced it with amalgam. The whole operation took two and a half hours.

'Now you're free. This tooth is healthier than it was. Man can perfect the universe, as we claim.' I didn't dare disagree, because I supposed that Dr Salem's action concealed something, that it was part of our 'mission'.

'Of course you don't owe me anything, not money nor gratitude: much more than that,' the dentist said finally with a frank and sonorous laugh. I began to worry.

During this time something terrible happened. I was transferred to Italy, where the incident with the Maestro took place.

I went back to my homeland, and when the risks of mortal disease in UR6 had faded once more, that molar which, as I have said, represented my religion, crumbled. There was no doubt, UR6 was dead, it had ceased to exist. I went to see Dr Taussig as though I was going to the scaffold. My knees trembled. I presented my case to the dentist, who worked for a long time, two hours at least, on the extraction of the tooth which represented all that my ancestors had passed down from one century to the next: the ancient wisdom, the ancient ardour of the faith, the ancient suffering. When he had finished, the silent dentist said to me: 'Congratulations, this tooth will never leave you at any price. It has split into ten parts, perhaps its cemented roots are still in the jawbone, and it will go everywhere with you, as roots often do.'

'The genius of creation!' I silently exclaimed. 'He's offering me a possible way out, when I'm reduced to a state of desperation! I shall tell this to Dr Kraus! I haven't lost my bet at all: I can ask for a special dispensation since the roots have stayed within me, and roots are everything!' I went home and immediately called Dr Kraus in Barcelona to tell him about the case.

'You can keep your roots,' the Spanish doctor said irritably, 'the important thing is that the tooth is no longer there. You won't be able to chew or defend yourself or defend your ideas. Accept it and stop looking for loopholes. Face up to reality. Only two teeth are in competition now, the sixth lower left and the fourth lower right (LL6 and LR4 *author's note*), the Muslim religion and the true one, my own.' Kraus wouldn't concede annulments, he demanded conversion!

I was preparing myself for this unpleasant event. It wasn't a very big deal. LL6 could receive the *coup de grâce* at any moment. To be honest, I didn't much care which religion I converted to: I was a faithless turncoat, who would betray his belief for money, a man without honour. Deep down I despised myself, and with myself everything that existed in the universe. But at that point something unexpected, mysterious and inexplicable occurred. I refer the reader to the story entitled 'Resilience'.

LL4

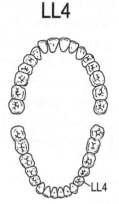

LL4

Another tangential story

Another tangential story is the one about a distant relative of mine, a second cousin, or great-uncle, I can't precisely define how closely related I was to him. I met him only on two occasions, and neither of the two meetings influenced the course of my life in the slightest, even if the second coincided with an event that was very important to me.

Let us move on. I met this cousin during my residence in Canada, on the occasion of the stipulation of an agreement between the government of my country and a newly established company devoted to the distribution of a new kind of taximeter. Maestro G. had planned a visit to a concert in Vancouver, and we were to remain in contact between

Toronto, Ottawa and, indeed, Vancouver. One day in Toronto
I saw an elderly man running through the suburban streets.
He was doing his daily run to stimulate his cardiac muscle and
was wearing only a green vest and black cotton shorts, identical to those that I wore as a schoolboy during gymnastics
lessons. Curiosity made me very forward: I stopped the man,
addressing him first in English and then in my own language.
Continuing to run on the spot – I found it really quite cold,
the people who lived there found it less so – the man replied
to me, pointing to the street I pretended I was looking for,
and then asked, in turn, how I had guessed where he came
from.

'It was the cotton shorts. I haven't seen shorts like those
since I was at school.'

'You're right. I've been wearing them for . . . fifty years.
After I left grammar school I never stopped wearing them
when I did my exercises. It's the only item of clothing I took
with me when I left our country.'

I asked him how long he had been living in Canada.

'So many years,' he answered, without being more precise.
There was subterfuge in his smile. 'And I still haven't got
used to it.'

'There's something very curious about this individual,' I
thought, allowing the conversation to slide towards a rendezvous the following afternoon. During our meeting, which
took place in a dreadful café, this man, in the course of three
interminable hours, told me the story of his life. I shall sum it
up in a few lines. Apart from anything, because it is not about
a life, rather the attempt to avoid it, to dodge its dangers. I
should say in passing that from what he said I understood

that he was a relative of mine, thrice removed. I embraced him and listened to his story, which consisted of curt phrases and silences. What follows is a summary.

Devoted and diligent as a child, this individual was so injured by and terrified of life that he quickly became an obedient servant to anyone who wanted to order him around: parents, brothers, schoolmates. Adventure was always far from his thoughts, and yet, during the years of the persecutions, he one day donned the hooded jacket worn by the mountain bands who assumed the name of the Swastika and, at the risk of being caught and having his throat cut, he crossed the town to warn his relations of a coming reprisal that he had learned about. He was twelve years old.

On another occasion, eleven years after the end of the war, he escaped from our small country, which had been invaded by the soldiers of a so-called friendly nation, wishing to preserve that 'friendship' by force.

Apart from those two episodes, nothing in particular appeared to have occurred in the life of our hero. He took his degree, began to teach, and fell ill with labyrinthitis to avoid having to continue teaching, since the fear that the children instilled in him made him detest the profession. After he was cured, as I have said, he fled his country and settled in Canada, where he undertook a course of studies without knowing which profession to follow, and then started to teach again. Another attack of labyrinthitis left him bedridden for six months; he got terrible vertigo just from sitting up. Once the illness had passed, he continued teaching, hating the Canadian schoolchildren more than he had ever hated those of his country of origin.

At the age of twenty-eight, to avoid being alone, he married a former fellow student. This woman, neither beautiful nor ugly, was a Canadian who dreamed of being an actress and dreamed about it all day, getting up at about two o'clock to see if her husband, coming back from school, had made her anything to eat, meeting with friends and lovers in the afternoon, flicking through magazines and going to the cinema and the theatre in the evening and at night. My distant relative spent twenty years looking after their two children, washing shirts, underwear, sheets, keeping the household going. At the age of fifty he divorced her. He then spent fifteen more years in a windowless apartment in the centre of Toronto, cultivating his passion for photographs that he collected in highly ordered albums. Rarely in his pictures did one see faces. Beneath the text 'my father' was a torso in a grey jacket, beneath 'my son' a back covered by the yellow waterproof worn by visitors to the Niagara Falls. It was hard to know whether the absurdity of these photographs was the result of a series of mistakes, or whether their author had wanted in some way to reduce the world to its insignificant details.

At the age of sixty-five my relative fell passionately in love. A thirty-year-old teacher, originally from Prague, beautiful and elegant, selected him as her victim. Married and the mother of a daughter, every year, on the pretext of going to see her parents, she set off with him across Austria and Switzerland, staying in little mountain pensions. After three weeks of the contemplative life, the couple would part and he, back in Canada, sat patiently day and night, sticking in newspaper cuttings and bad photographs, waiting for the phone to ring and for her to greet him with a conspiratorial whisper.

He wanted news of his children and his brothers and sisters by the most indirect route: it was too dangerous to maintain personal contact with them.

That is what I gleaned from his reminiscences that day.

The second time I saw him was at home, while I was going to Tobacco Street to have Dr Metzger remove LL4, a premolar that had never given me any trouble. It hadn't ever been carious, it had remained intact, white, surrounded by teeth that were holed and patched, beheaded, blackened, mobile. Like my cousin or great-uncle, who had made titanic efforts to avoid life's dangers, that tooth had been saved from all kinds of storms. And yet, during the afternoon of my second meeting with that man, LL4 was taken out and thrown in the rubbish. There was no longer any point to it, so it became an irritation, preventing, along with my other two or three remaining teeth, the introduction of a healthy set of dentures. So sparing myself, then, seeking desperately to save myself from pain – had it all been pointless if something could be torn from you anyway? Try as I might I couldn't decide.

The extraction was not easy; Dr Metzger had to do a lot of preliminary work before he could extract the premolar. An irregularity in the roots produced an unusually solid attachment. I felt no pain, but the dentist's agitation alarmed me. In the end, after about three-quarters of an hour, it was all finished. In the mean time my thoughts returned more than once to the Canadian relative I had just seen again.

'What brings you here?' he had asked me. The question was becoming more and more worrying, as it happens, and this tangential story had also become central to my life. In what way?

When she met this relative, Rachel, who came with me to the dentist, became agitated and distracted. She kept asking the Canadian insistently what he had been up to and how he was keeping. All of a sudden, whilst under the knife, I was struck by a ridiculous suspicion. It occurred to me that on the earlier occasion, during my mission to Canada, I had also been accompanied by my wife, and that one evening she had taken a walk with my cousin or great-uncle or whatever he was. During the walk, they had been to see his windowless apartment. For days afterwards, Rachel had talked to me endlessly about that man who, in her eyes, had understood the true essence of existence, and who had, in the face of life, reduced all his own needs to nothing. Rachel had been inordinately impressed by this art of reduction. Quite suddenly, while the dentist was drilling my tooth, I was seized by a terrible jealousy. I almost wanted to halt the operation just to check that she, having left me at the dentist's to go and buy some anti-haemorrhage medication for my bleeding gums, hadn't gone in search of that monster instead. The moment I rose from the dentist's chair I saw her sitting, smiling and peaceful, in the waiting room. The door was open: Rachel had just returned and wanted to see how far we had progressed.

After this I never asked any questions of my wife. At our age it would have been ridiculous, but I couldn't swear that my Rachel, the living image of fidelity and devotion, didn't take the briefest of vacations from her own solid unhappiness while we were in Canada.

RESILIENCE

Resilience is defined by the capacity of an object or a material to withstand the sudden demands made upon a particular part of it. These are not static demands such as traction, compression or incision, but dynamic demands, such as impact. In order to test the resilience of an object or a body, an apparatus called a Charpy pendulum is used. It consists of a pillar with a hinged arm at the end of which is a hammer with a rounded blade. At the other end of the pillar is the object under examination, positioned on the trajectory of the hammer during the latter's fall. Resilience is the relation between the energy required for the breakage of the object and its diameter S.

$$R = \frac{pH - ph}{S}$$

Where H is the original height of the hammer, h its rebound height, S the diameter of the object to be broken, p the weight of the hammer.

The filling Dr Salem had applied two years previously to my first lower left molar LL6 had suddenly broken. The material used had clearly had a resilience incapable of resisting the impact of mastication: thus, after a few months, a crack had formed in the filling. There would have been no point, now, in subjecting that material to the hardness tests of Martens or Brinell, or the celebrated Austrian Mohs (1773–1839), based on resistance to cracks: LL6 had a terrible crack in its side, and the filling had to be completely redone. Of course, I had to tell Dr Kraus, without whose permission I could not even have cleaned one of the two teeth surviving from our bet. For days I sought that elusive medic: I was unable to contact him either by letter or by phone. In the end I was happy about this: my tongue was beginning to get used to the internal roughness of the hole (I could have used a rugosimeter or profilometer, but what would have been the point?).

'Have you thought of having the molar filled?' Rachel asked me from time to time.

'I don't see why I should,' I replied, more irritated with myself than with her.

One night at about two o'clock the phone rang. 'It's Dr Kraus,' Rachel whispered to me, handing me the receiver. 'He's here, he wants to see you, he's calling from the casino.'

I spoke to him. He was asking me for a small loan, having lost everything at *chemin de fer.*

I was very surprised by this sudden, strange message, but I hurried to get dressed, walked to the nearest taxi rank and tried to find him. The First District was deserted. I went into the hotel that housed the big gaming rooms, and soon found him among the sleepy and rumpled foreign gamblers.

'What on earth brings you here?'

'And you, what on earth brings you here?' replied Kraus with his dentist's smile.

'I don't know. I felt I ought to come and help you.'

He asked me for a few dollars and, taking advantage of the fact that I knew one of the croupiers, a second cousin of my wife's, I gave it to him. I was about to bid him farewell – our challenge was bound by a tacit agreement of mutual assistance – when he suddenly put a hand on my arm and whispered: 'And your molar? What state is it in? Has the crucial point arrived or not?'

I told him what had happened and scolded him for not having been somewhere I could find him, preventing me from intervening to save LL6.

'I'm sorry, I was travelling. So is your molar almost lost? Show me.'

'Whatever are you thinking of?' I stammered. 'Here, in front of everybody . . .'

'Where's the harm in it. I'm a dentist,' Kraus insisted. In the end I went along with him and showed him LL6, at the back of my mouth.

'It's horrible!' I exclaimed. 'There's massive decay. Do you think you can save the tooth?'

'I don't know,' he said, shaking his head. 'No, it can't be done,' Kraus went on. 'The tooth is done for. I'll extract it myself, if you like. And I'll construct a nice fixed-movable bridge for you.'

'What does that mean?' I asked.

'It's a bridge made with one fixed part cemented to the abutment of the tooth and one removable part which generally includes the false tooth. And after that let's talk about the salvation of your soul and your spirit.'

At this point our conversation took a sudden, worrying turn. When I calmly said that it was time now to bring the silly joke to an end, he looked at me seriously and asked if I wanted to retract my word, spoken and written.

'Yes,' I answered, raising my head.

'You can't,' Kraus whispered between his teeth.

'Why? There's no official obligation in that contract, or rather there is, but only for you,' I said, ludicrously self-confident.

'I know. But if you retract your word, I am authorized to kill you. I'll do it light-heartedly, as though calling in a debt.'

'What?' I stammered.

'Yes. If you don't keep your word and don't carry out the abjuration of your faith, I'll kill you. That's always been the sense of the bet as far as I was concerned.'

I had never before found myself in such a situation, I had never received such an explicit threat. I have always been an insignificant figure, the empty outline cut from the fabric of events. Why this sudden violence towards me?

The dentist prevented any further reflection on my part: he wanted to console me immediately. 'If you do everything we have agreed, I will pay your ticket from here to Barcelona, I will put you up in a luxury hotel, treat all your diseased teeth for free, and in the end you will have the sum you already know about. You, in return, will have to betray the thing that is dearest to you, that vast entity that envelops you along with millions of other human beings. What shall we call it? Faith? But you will have to pursue a different destiny from that day onwards.'

The course of my destiny was about to be determined by three teeth: for weeks I couldn't free myself of that thought. And my resilience was about to be reduced to zero, the hammer was about to fall on my head from a height H. My departure for Barcelona was only a few weeks or months away: after UR6, LL6 could be extracted at any moment.

On one of those days, at around three o'clock in the afternoon, Maestro G. called me. 'Do you never read the papers? I'm giving a concert this evening, didn't you know?'

A series of expletives in Italian and in my own language reminded me that friendship knows no limits of any kind. In the past we had consented to be each other's murderers, but that couldn't weaken the bond between us.

'So, are you coming this evening, yes or no?' asked the Maestro solemnly. I made my excuses and said I had to call my wife and my daughter. Rachel, who was listening in to the conversation by leaning on me and putting her ear to the receiver, was making eloquent gestures in the negative. But I, like Don Giovanni talking to the stone statue, replied: 'I'm coming!'

I went to the concert and nothing suspicious happened. The Maestro made no secret sign to me, he sent me no letters or parcels, he didn't communicate anything that might have been considered compromising. The moment I saw him in his dressing room after the concert I told him what was bothering me: the outcome of the bet and Kraus's threat.

'What? You're telling me that you've breezily agreed to the insulting ceremony that consigned so many of your people to the flames four hundred years ago? Are you giving up an intimate part of your being just like that?' the Maestro asked, taking off his dress shirt, which was drenched in sweat.

'I can't do otherwise. I'm sure that lunatic will find some way of killing me,' I answered.

'He already has done. You're dead now. You've entered the flow, and it isn't going to give you up. And there's something else behind it as well; the decree comes from a higher authority than that miserable dentist.'

'From whom?' I murmured, terrified. He must know something, given that he had, in his turn, been the one who was supposed to carry out a similar 'decree'.

'From much higher up than you think. And now tell me, what do you want of me?' The Maestro was drying his back and his hair.

'Actually, you were the one who called me,' I ventured.

'That's just appearance. Really you're the one looking for me, you want me to make your decisions for you, isn't that right?' The Maestro stopped in front of me and looked me in the eye. 'I could calmly give you the worst advice, do you realize that?'

'Yes, but I hope you won't.' I was aware of a note of servile pleading in my voice.

'Fine. Now, off you go. Can you hear how many people

there are outside the dressing room? They all want my auto-graph.'

I felt obliged to congratulate him again. 'The *William Tell* Overture was magnificent. Thank you for that. And the third movement of the Seventh . . .' I said a deferential goodbye and left the dressing room. Running down dark streets, I breathed in the air, which smelt of coal. Here and there drunks were asleep on the footpath, old ladies with incredibly bent legs and threadbare, greasy coats walked in front of me. I reached the Eighth District. 'The time has come,' I thought. 'It would have to be as dark as this.'

Rachel and the children were already asleep. I sat down in the kitchen and wrote on a squared sheet of paper the list of objects and clothes that I was going to take to Spain with me.

I didn't have the caries filled: LL6 began to move in its socket, and I was now a condemned man. I had decided to take advantage of Kraus's offer to undertake the extraction and the construction of the bridge. In two exchanges of letters we agreed the date on which I was to leave. I was now in a pos-ition to go anywhere, at any time: in Europe one no longer seemed to be confined between one country and another, and in any case I no longer had any reason for taking official jour-neys abroad. When there were only three days to go, and I was still contemplating the idea of suicide, I received a letter from Barcelona. It didn't bear the printed letterhead of the dental surgery. Who could it be from? I opened the envelope, and among the three white sheets folded over several times, I found a newspaper cutting in which I recognized Dr Kraus's photo-graph. The article dwelt at length on his career, the mysterious things that had happened to his family, the suspicions that he might be a member of the Russian secret service. Finally, an account of his suicide. He had shot himself with a revolver at six o'clock in the morning the previous week. He had had visitors the previous evening, and throughout the night his neighbours had heard exclamations and curses interspersed with long periods of silence. The only voice to be heard was unmistakably that of the dentist, and no one else.

I felt as I had done when I was a child, inspired by life and a sense of harmony with the universe. After a few weeks I started to become aware of the void in my existence, and the absence of any threat that might have given it a meaning. I acquiesced in that void, adapting to my life with Rachel in my miserable lodging on Via Karpfenstein. I had LL6 extracted, while the last survivor of the bet, LR4, remained in its place.

Three years later I had my final visit from the Maestro. One morning in December he had come to our house unannounced. I had difficulty recognizing him. He hadn't been conducting for some time and was living in his house near Cortina d'Ampezzo in the Dolomites. Every now and again he came to see his old friends, to recall past adventures. In contemporary Europe, crisscrossed with wars and secessions, he found nothing of interest, nothing notable in comparison to earlier decades. And yet even the resilience of our own time had been reduced to nothing, the apparent order had broken.

'Nothing has any meaning any longer, the world has said everything there is to be said. This is only the obvious, the ordinary epilogue,' the Maestro repeated. We invited him to dinner and he was delighted to eat in such modest surroundings: splendour annoyed him.

'And your bet with that curious dentist, how did that turn out? With an *auto-da-fé*?' he asked suddenly.

'No. I didn't need to do anything in the end.' I told him what had happened. Suddenly in his smile I thought I sensed something unthinkable. He had killed that dentist, he had wanted to save my life at all costs, just as I had saved his! I asked him if he had eliminated Kraus.

'What can I tell you?' the Maestro asked abruptly. 'I went to Kraus for treatment and challenged him to a game of poker. We played all night, in the presence of two witnesses. He shouted, he cursed, he suffered, but he lost. He lost everything he had. I won everything that belonged to him. He seemed destroyed by anxiety, but happy! Happy! He had finally lost the game. Then I reminded him of his bet with you. What was he going to give, in exchange for your abjuration, now that he no longer owned anything? He roused himself from his disastrous happiness. "I've been an idiot!" he said over and over again. Then he begged me to grant him one more game. "I'm sure I'll win everything back if you allow me one more game. Otherwise I'll be forced to kill myself." I conceded nothing. I left, and he repeated that hackneyed old gesture of the gambler: he killed himself at dawn.'

The Maestro wasn't joking, and after this he disappeared again for a number of years.

Around this time Dr Metzger reduced LR4 to a mere stump, and shortly thereafter he made preparations for my fixed-movable bridge.

UL4

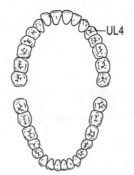

UL4

The consequences of dignity

My acquaintance with Dr Leonardo Leonardi began in the context of my discovery of what we call the dignity of pain. Sometimes, in hospitals or on buses, I had seen the opaque, intense expression of people who had decided to hide their physical suffering from the eyes of others. I have always wondered about the reason for that pointless effort, since pain itself is unashamed to move from one part of the body to another, to make its presence felt in our various organs. Pain is immodest. Perhaps if we wished to resist it we could do so with the same sense of modesty and guilt with which we hide our own nakedness. But perhaps pain is also the emissary of the One who wishes to demonstrate, through his intermediary, the power he holds over us.

Dr Leonardi, a dentist recommended to me by the cultural attaché of our embassy in the Eternal City, was very sensitive to the suffering of others. 'The minute you feel any pain, please shout. I hate the idea that I might be torturing my fellow humans.'

'In that case you should have chosen a different profession!' I thought, not daring to say it. I exposed UL4 and told him that the amalgam filling I had been given forty years before had fallen out the previous evening, during an embassy dinner to celebrate the great political transformations that had taken place in my country.

'Ah, amalgam!' exclaimed the dentist, with his jutting chin and square face. 'Even today it's the best material for fillings. Unfortunately it contains mercury, and mercury is a poison. You've been sucking poison for forty years, with this filling in your mouth.'

All of a sudden I felt ill. 'Poison!' I exclaimed. I wanted to have all my teeth that had been filled with amalgam extracted, but realized that that would leave me almost entirely toothless.

'Yes, poison,' Leonardi insisted. 'But, by way of consolation, I can tell you that the materials used today are almost certainly carcinogenic. Choose between tumours and kidney failure.'

Setting these unpleasant subjects aside, he began to examine me. He looked at the tooth that had been left unfilled and explained that before applying a white resin to the stump he would have to enlarge the hole a little. 'The minute you feel any pain, shriek, if you please,' he repeated. He reached for the bur. The mere sound of it alarmed me and sent me retreating inside myself.

'Don't be afraid, you won't feel a thing. I'll be careful. I have such a high opinion of your culture that I would rather stick the bur in my own eye than cause pain to any of you.'

With the buzzing instrument in his hand he started listing the names of great architects, writers, musicians, born that century between Austria and my homeland. 'In two thousand years such a concentration of superior minds has occurred only in the Renaissance and Ancient Greece.'

Suddenly two thousand years struck me as a ridiculous length of time compared to the age of the universe, estimated at about fifteen billion years. 'Yes, yes, I'm proud to come from that part of the world,' I said.

'Actually,' the dentist went on, 'it was the people who appeared so civilized who unleashed the most terrifying barbarities. Could those two things be compatible, spiritual greatness and the urge to destroy? Or is the latter the consequence of the former? But now we're returning to the dualism of the mind and the brain, to what is called "the revolution of consciousness", a "top-down" relation from mind to molecule. The consciousness oversees and holds back wars, genocide, the impulses of chaotic forces. I have too much admiration for the Karlsplatz underground stations, *Transfigured Night*, *The Kiss*, *Andreas, and the United Ones*.'

He leaned the drill into the cavity of UL4, and suddenly an appalling pain reached my brain. 'You have to resist!' my brain shrieked inside me. 'As a representative and an heir of that great culture you must resist!'

But Dr Leonardo plunged his bur even further in. 'I beg you, scream for the love of God,' murmured the dentist leaning over me.

I appreciated the delicacy of this Mediterranean gentleman, his horror of pain. 'Yes, do feel free to scream, don't be
ashamed,' the dentist whispered again, but perhaps he knew
by now that I wouldn't, that according to the laws of the
north pain had to be borne in silence by force of mind, lest
it disturb the harmony of the world. Dignity is a terrible sentence from which southern man, in his ancient wisdom, is
often able to extricate himself. That much we know: out-
ward silence masks the most fearsome hubbub of
consciousness, the higher authority controlling the atoms of
pain.

At a certain point, something in UL4 snapped, probably
the last layer of dentine: blinding flashes jerked through me,
twinges coming direct from my brain and my heart, from my
lungs and my kidneys, from my anus, from the whole of my
being. I didn't scream. 'Not too bad,' said Dr Leonardi, 'I
thought I'd hit the nerve. Instead I'm going to have to go on
drilling for a bit. Go on, relax for a moment.'

I was having difficulty breathing, I was stunned. 'We're like
worms, they skewer us and it's all over,' I thought.

Dr Leonardi then started reciting from memory, in
German, sentences from *The Man Without Qualities*. 'What an
era, what minds, so unlike the Latin civilization!' he finally
exclaimed. 'And here, within those few square miles of central Europe, the modern world came into being.'

He finished cleaning the cavity with movements that
seemed to me immeasurably slow, something like the rate of
one movement every fifteen billion years. 'Pain is the world's
clock,' I thought. Dr Leonardi prepared the filling made with
a slightly rough, perhaps porous resin. All of a sudden, while

he was smoothing the material with a strip of transparent paper, he began to curse the world into which he had been born, its pettiness and superficiality.

'Sometimes I feel like filling my crash helmet with TNT – I ride a motorbike – driving down to the Quirinale Palace, butting a guard of honour in the stomach and sending everything sky high: the president of the republic, his palace, his cars, all the marble, the gold, the horses and, of course, myself. I'm fed up with my patients, with my studies. Respectable men come to me after discovering love at the age of fifty, and my brain echoes with their screams and their amorous tales, elderly, hypersensitive men who, at the first touch, jump from the dentist's chair, without dignity, without restraint. Then there's that other great invention of our Mediterranean world: the family. Your wife, your children oppress you, suffocate you, flay you. What's it all for, eh?'

Despite an unbearable pain in the tooth he had just filled, my dignity prevented me from screaming. 'It's just a bit sensitive there,' I ventured to say.

'Oh you poor thing, why didn't you say?' the dentist exclaimed. From a grey cupboard he took a rubber tube with a metallic tip, which he leaned against my cheek, at the spot corresponding to the premolar UL4. 'These are laser rays, they're made of agitated electrons; no one knows why, but they take the pain away. Try it, just hold the tube for ten minutes, press it against your cheek. It'll do you good, you'll see.'

I obeyed, and he started complaining about his wife. 'I left home six months ago. I couldn't bear it any more. Yeah, and the other day I saw my wife in the street, the traffic was terrible. "Why don't you kill her by crashing your bike into

her?" I asked myself. I was about to accelerate when the
bloody woman throws herself behind a passer-by. Bitch! How
did you manage to let her know you wanted her dead? She
always manages to get away! Like last year, in America. We
were about to go swimming in the Pacific Ocean, and a massive wave swallowed her up. "Drown, I beg you!" I screamed,
but somehow she got out of the water, half dead. "I'm half
dead," she said. "Why only half?" I asked, and she murmured
one of those insipid phrases she comes out with. I hurled
myself at her throat. "Give it another go!" I yelled, and she
started crying. How disgusting and undignified of the woman,
so unlike the great Roman civilization!'

I listened to him in terror. 'Maybe he's trying to kill me
too, with that laser contraption,' I thought. 'The man's a vir-
tual murderer.'

'Don't think ill of me, I beg you,' the dentist went on. 'I
work out these homicidal thoughts during the long afternoons I spend here, bent over the mouths – the sewers,
rather – of the worst kind of bourgeoisie. Listen, maybe you
can help me . . .' he said, suddenly smiling. 'You must be married, and no doubt you hate your wife. We could swap
favours. You kill my wife, I'll kill yours. If you hit the target,
I'll treat you for the rest of your life, for as long as your teeth
last, and they're pretty sound, apart from periodontitis and
caries. So, what do you say?' He started laughing like a man
unhinged. 'I hope you understand the joke. You lot have had
some comedians in your time! The English pale in comparison.'

I never went back to Dr Leonardi, and was happy to be out
of his clutches. His reconstruction of UL4, in any case, was

hammered to pieces two years later by Dr Metzger in my homeland. Dr Leonardi had left germs in the tooth cavity and they had caused a granuloma. The filling was remade, but during the operation I felt no pain since Dr Leonardi had accidentally killed the nerve with his drill. Very soon the tooth became mobile, and every now and again I would take it between thumb and index finger to test its solidity. This operation brought me all kinds of pleasure, carnal and spiritual, the pleasure of the baser realms of matter, and that of the peaks of the mind, the spirit.

One day, when I was sixty-five and my son Gerson had finally graduated in chemical engineering at the age of thirty-five, I had a sudden impulse to remove that wobbly tooth on my own. I resisted the pain with dignity and carried out my plan. A month later I was appointed commercial attaché at our embassy in Rome. I took the tooth with me, and one fine May morning I went in search of Dr Leonardi with the premolar in my briefcase. I wanted to show him what our dentistry was like, unlike his own. But Dr Leonardi had moved to Patagonia five years previously, and no one had heard a word from him since. 'It's not enough to have given pain,' I murmured on the threshold of his surgery, 'they also give us the dignity to put up with it. Pain and dignity are our worst curse.' The dentist's old wife nodded.

LL7

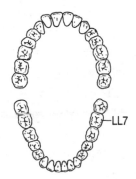

—LL7

Galvanic pain
(First story of senile love)

The affliction of LL7, the second lower left molar, has for a long time been symbolic for me of the torment of consciousness. Love and knowledge have this in common: the mystery and pain of deprivation.

LL7 began to give me pain a few days after I met Livia, an actress of about thirty, in one of the television offices. She was blonde with green eyes, tall, elegant, serious and gentle, at least in appearance. The opposite of my wife Rachel, in a sense, who was brunette, squat, graceless and cheerful.

Livia had come to talk about something she had planned with a director in the department of classic dramas. She was to interpret the role of the cruel Lady Macbeth in a television version of Shakespeare's drama.

'Where will we find the right expression for such an evil and ambitious character?' I wondered. Then I remembered the famous mad scene and asked myself the opposite question: 'How can such an evil being also harbour gentleness and remorse? Who could have inspired Shakespeare to paint such a bold portrait of femininity?'

On that occasion we barely greeted one another, but a few days later she returned to see my colleague and friend, and we went for tea. LL7 began to give me pain after the first sip. I immediately went to see Dr Taussig who carried out the simple filling in less than no time: given the limited extent of the caries, the cavity was prepared according to Gabel's criteria, with proximal walls and convergent vestibules. The material employed was amalgam.

The third time I met Livia was in the street. It was snowing, with sparse but persistent flakes, and there was a festive mood in the city. Once more I offered her tea, and this time I did a lot of talking about myself, because I wanted a particular image of myself to be imprinted on her mind. I was very excited, and so attracted to her that I could do nothing about it. I was familiar with this state, and knew that it led first to confusion, then to bleakness.

'You've really been around the place, haven't you!' said Livia, after listening to me for a long time. Her face bore an expression of inviting melancholy.

'Not quite enough if I haven't met you before now,' I said, with a stupid smile that seemed to be stamped on my face, and which I could imagine in my mind's eye.

Two evenings later I found myself in Livia's little apartment in the Thirteenth District. 'And do you think you've arrived somewhere now?' she asked, with a smile that was a little sad but still inviting.

'Yes.'

I was sincere. I thought I had found that absolute otherness, that completely different being that I had never found in the women or men I had known until then. I was entering the unknown.

While we were making love, in a remote village in central Asia vast reserves of energy were being unleashed, the terrifying force of matter was beginning to expand as heat and poison. Radioactive particles began to fly across Europe, to be deposited on animals, plants, water, mountains, threatening mankind with illnesses, deaths, genetic deformities, the births of monsters.

'Who could have ordained such a disaster?' Livia asked me the following day, when we met up in a café on Circular Street.

'I don't know,' I said. 'I'm sure it isn't chance, and that like everything that happens to us it's just a sign.'

'Everything? Even our love?' asked Livia.

She believed in the immunity of love. And what about the lies I told Rachel and the children? And the ones she told her husband, who had gone to Germany to perform an operetta?

In the midst of this disaster Maestro G. arrived to conduct his most ambitious concert: Verdi's *Requiem*. As a conductor he was no match for this music, as we both knew, but I revered him none the less because he too was everything that I was not, and yet at the same time he was like me. Creative imagination and a life in music had lifted him to a sphere of greatness even if, like myself, he was small and insignificant.

'Why has all this happened?' I asked him before the concert.

'The message is clear, even if the manner in which it is conveyed is a terrible one,' answered the Maestro. 'Don't ask questions. This evening I'm conducting the *Requiem*. Do you think it's coincidence that they've asked me to conduct the *Requiem* this evening of all evenings, and here of all places?'

Only a few years later, when the world had changed absolutely, did I understand. It really had been a most fateful sign.

'And what if my embraces with Livia are merely signs?' I asked myself. 'What if everything's a fiction, a lie? Lies and fictions are life's worst phantoms. My whole life has been crisscrossed with them, my whole life a battle against them.'

The evening of the concert I found Confucius' *Dialogues* on the Maestro's table. He had borrowed it from me, but perhaps he had returned it to give me the *coup de grâce*.

The following day, sitting in Dr Taussig's antechamber, I started flicking through the book. On page thirty I read: 'Master Kung Fu-tzu said to Pei Chu: "The most difficult thing to achieve is perfect sincerity. I have never known anyone who had achieved it, not even I myself have achieved it entirely, never."'

The sentence set me thinking. I swore to renounce all fictions. The tooth that the doctor had just treated, LL7, was giving me a great deal of pain, and that was why I was there. So I accused the dentist of having irritated the nerve in my molar. Had I not read that sentence I would never have dared deliver such a reproach to a dentist I considered my superior. The dentist denied all responsibility.

'I've been a dentist for thirty years. I have never caused

infections or inflammations in any of my patients,' said Taussig, piqued. He was a tall man, with thick, sleek hair, his face flaccid and hairless. At this point he had one heart attack behind him. After giving the tooth a thorough examination, he came to the conclusion that I must have a cold as that was the only way he could account for the pain. He prescribed an analgesic and sent me on my way. I took the pills for a few days and felt better.

The pain returned to LL7 three evenings later, the moment Livia burst into tears. This was her way of expressing the apotheosis of erotic pleasure. Obviously, the analgesic stopped the pain but not its cause. I returned to Dr Taussig, who had already applied two gold crowns to two of my molars (see p. 199 ff.). He now prescribed a partial X-ray of the lower left semi-arch, for which I had to stand in several interminable queues. A week later I went back to see him with the X-rays, which showed no decay and no aberration apart from that which existed already: my many fillings, the precarious nature of the bone, the two bridges. Taussig then prescribed a panoramic X-ray that took another week of bureaucratic queuing.

In the meantime I went on seeing Livia in her petit-bourgeois apartment, full of knick-knacks and dolls in folk costume, and making love with her, despite the searing pains in my lower left molar, to the accompaniment of her uncontrollable weeping.

'Do you feel at home when you're with me?' she asked.

'Yes. I feel I've arrived where I wanted to be.'

'So why don't you get divorced?' she said gently, looking at me with her big green eyes.

'Because . . .' I wanted to be sincere and tell her that despite having 'been around' so much, I had a horror of change, and immobility was paradise as far as I was concerned. I didn't say it.

'I'll think about it,' I stammered, 'I'll think about it.'

In the weeks and months that followed, the request became more pressing and for the third time I was on the point of leaving my family for ever. By now my toothache tormented me every day, so I decided to have LL7 extracted, or all my teeth, if necessary, just to bring the pain to an end. It was Livia who took me to her personal dentist, Dr Fink in the Second District, and asked the stout blond medic to proceed – just so as to liberate me – to the slaughter. Perhaps there was a hint of malice in the request, because of my continual delays making any decision about the divorce. This dentist, alien as far as I was concerned to everything that belonged to my world, managed to preserve my teeth.

'I think I've understood,' he said after examining my oral cavity, 'that what we have here is a classic case of galvanic pain.'

'And what might that be?'

'The last two upper left molars are crowned with gold. This tooth,' he tapped LL7 with the handle of the probe, 'is filled with amalgam. An electric circuit has grown up between the mercury of the amalgam and the gold of the crown. Every time you press your jaws together you provoke an electric charge. When you hold your mouth closed, the charges are continuous. It's as if you were sitting in an electric chair, except that the power of the circuit established between your teeth is obviously much weaker. Whoever filled the second-last lower molar, or crowned the two last upper left molars, didn't realize this. Galvanic pain is rare, but modern dentistry is certainly aware of it.'

'Damn you, Taussig! You'll pay for that some day! You've made me suffer for months and months,' I exclaimed silently. I started planning my revenge – so much suffering cried out for vengeance. I put it off until a few months hence.

The replacement of amalgam in the filling of LL7 with some resin or polymer stopped the galvanic pain as if by magic, and it also stopped the furious desire I felt for Livia. We parted in violent circumstances. I was slapped roundly by the gentle blonde actress, who revealed herself that evening as a truly bloody Lady Macbeth: even her voice lowered to resemble a man's. Everything between us was as ghostly as the electricity that had been circulating in my jaw for months, from one tooth to another, until Dr Fink killed the phantom by replacing the filling. Banquo's ghost, in short, was fatal to Macbeth and the cruel Lady Macbeth.

It would be superfluous to say that I didn't achieve the sincerity I so yearned for; throughout the whole episode I never spoke of it to Rachel. The lie would not let me rest and in desperation, even as I lied, I consoled myself with the fact that not even the great Confucius had ever managed to attain the ideal of perfect sincerity.

As to the pain, I admitted that it had been necessary in order to deepen my knowledge of physics, of myself and of the arts of dentistry.

DEPOSITION OF DOCTOR TAUSSIG

Fifteen years ago I sued a dentist. Recently I rediscovered, at the back of my desk, a photocopy of the minutes of the trial. I reproduce several pages from it here. I am struck by how combative I was in those days. I couldn't do it today.

I met S.G. in the spring some years ago, at exactly half-past three on 21 April. The appointment was for three o'clock, but S.G. arrived half an hour late. When I remonstrated with him, he asserted that he was accustomed to turning up late for all his appointments and that there was nothing he could do about it, it was something stronger than his will, perhaps it was a form of neurosis, perhaps a fear of his fellow man, perhaps both.

'Then you should see a psychiatrist,' I replied, but he
looked at me with an expression of such pain that my irritation melted away. I ushered him into my surgery and
examined him. The two upper left molars showed clear signs
of phlogosis with swellings of the gums and cheek. Very
extensive caries, long neglected, had so far jeopardized the
pulp as to suggest that the pathological process might be
resolved only by extraction. As far as I could see those teeth
could be saved. For life, for a semblance of life, you have to
fight to the bitter end. That thought has always been the
driving force behind my work as a dentist, and even today I
remain of the same opinion. In the case of S.G., however, I
had to try absolutely everything. In that particular place I
could apply only a removable prosthesis, not a fixed one. But
for only two teeth it didn't strike me as appropriate to resort
to that kind of intervention, especially since the patient was
still relatively young.

I scrupulously explained all this to my new patient, and
outlined the treatment required if the two molars were to be
salvaged.

Given that some pulp still remained, and that the caries was
in the occlusal and in the vestibular surfaces, the two teeth
needed to be filed down before the gold crowns could be
applied.

Hearing this word, the patient gave a start. 'Gold?' he
asked. 'Did I hear you correctly?'

I reassured him. 'Are you in financial difficulties? I'll give
you an estimate, and then you can decide in your own time.'

Once again, S.G. made a pitiful impression upon me. I am
sensitive to social issues, I've been a member of the Party for

twenty years. I asked him what he did for a living and learned that S.G. worked in television. I promised him that we could come to an arrangement and fixed the first appointment for a week later. S.G. went off looking like a beaten dog, I can't think how else to put it.

He turned up for the appointment forty minutes late, bringing down upon my head the furious reproaches of the next patient, who was a stout and aggressive lady. Without a preamble, S.G. told me my estimate was too much for him, and so he had no option but to abandon the operation. But before investigating the subject any further, he made a suggestion. If I would apply the two gold crowns free of charge, he would give me half an hour's television airtime in a scientific slot, thus bringing me a huge amount of publicity. He asked me whether I had introduced any innovations in the field of dentistry, whether I had invented new systems of treatment or anything of that kind. I told him about the curved titanium implants prepared on the model of real roots, which, because of their shape, are less easily rejected by the bone than straight implants or platinum plates. S.G. showed a great deal of interest in my invention, and assured me that he would do everything he could to enable me to take part in a television programme.

Vanity and greed have been the ruin of so many lofty spirits, and I too, trusting in S.G.'s repeated promises, fell into the same trap. I carried out the operation I have just described without demanding any financial remuneration, and applied the two gold crowns to the seventh and eighth teeth in the upper jaw. After the final session, S.G. said a few things to me which so impressed me that I remember them to this day.

'Last week I was in Prague. In an antique shop window I saw some gold crowns taken from someone's teeth. What an obscenity! I was horrified at the sight of those empty crowns, I felt I had been exposed to a sick joke. I shuddered at the idea that such a futile impression of life could remain intact, while I would vanish into the void. Me!'

Today, with full hindsight, I can confidently state that this horror was the purest fiction, a tale invented to distract my attention from the deceit to which I was about to fall victim. Despite S.G.'s repeated promises, those television 'shoots' in which I was supposed to take part never took place, and I found myself defrauded of three or four grams of gold and the proceeds of a professional loan. The damages accruing to my person from this situation I shall discuss elsewhere. Here I wish only to reaffirm that S.G.'s accusation of professional incompetence, and the report to this effect made to this tribunal derive from these suppositions and no others, and that the accused should be S.G. and not myself.

I enclose copies of the numerous requests for payments, all of which regularly remained unanswered. I have nothing further to add here except to say that if I were to listen to other individuals of this type I could not devote myself to my most precious social duty without the help of a lawyer.

SUMMARY OF MY DEPOSITION

I went to Dr Taussig for the treatment of my two last upper molars in the left arch on the advice of Dr Sperber. The appointment was arranged not for 21 April but for 13 May, I remember this most precisely, because on that same morning there was a violent attack on a world-famous figure. This attack resulted in a pistol being fired into the buttocks of the designated victim, and I believe that this was not due to chance but to the infallible aim of the marksman; that was how it was supposed to be, and that was how it was. A few weeks previously I found myself in the Dolomites in the company of Maestro G., whom I am honoured to consider a very dear friend. This artist who, despite his global fame, does not scorn to work in our country for notoriously low fees, this great Italian musician who shares our social ideals and fights on their behalf, was my delightful host and guide only a few days before my teeth became carious. We had been in the snows of the Dolomites, the two of us alone, our sole means of communication a walkie-talkie that the Maestro took with him wherever he went.

In the course of these long excursions we discussed many profound topics that I could list for you, but that would not be relevant to this trial. To give you some idea, though, of the level of our talks, I might mention the issue of randomness in art, the existence or otherwise of chance, of music as a universal language signifying nothing, and so on.

One day we set about climbing the Falzarego. I have always found this mountain if not exactly hostile, at least forbidding. I considered it, and still view it today, as an enormous foreign body in the planetary tissue of cities, landscapes and water, something that places obstacles between man and .   but these reflections have no place in a courtroom either.

From time to time Maestro G. communicated via his walkie-talkie with some friend or relative, and I listened to his excited speeches without understanding a word, but

enjoying the music of Italian, that most beautiful of languages.

At the end of that unforgettable week, while climbing the
Falzarego, the Maestro and I were approached by policemen,
known as *carabinieri*, who proceeded to arrest us and keep us
in prison unjustly for over a month. It was during those terrible days that the two teeth in question began to give me
pain. My cheek swelled up to an inordinate extent, and looking at myself in the water of the washbasin I saw the image of
Neanderthal man rather than that of S.G., the son of the
Schächter of the Seventh District. This transformation had ren-
dered me almost unrecognizable, and the Italian authorities
who held us under arrest had great trouble resolving the issue
of my identity. In the end, our country's government took
official steps and I was released. When, at about midnight
one night, I knocked on the door of my house, my wife and
my children didn't recognize me. After listening to the story
of my hardships they wept for a long time. The next day I
went to see Dr Sperber and he, by now tired of the whole
thing, referred me to Dr Taussig: this decided the fate of my
two molars.

I can only repeat what I declared when I made my original
complaint, to the effect that I had just identified myself as
someone who worked in television when Dr Taussig started
trying to bribe me, offering his own professional services free
of charge in return for an appearance on one of our television
programmes. He wanted to show the viewers the advantages
of his curved titanium implant with a fixed dental prosthesis
mounted upon it.

Of course I refused his offer, apart from anything because,

in all sincerity, I had insufficient authority to keep such a promise. Anyway, during the sessions that followed, Dr Taussig continued to insist, offering me not only treatment free of charge, but two gold crowns. In the mean time the swelling in my face had subsided and, thinking once more about the transformation I had just undergone, I reached the conclusion that teeth are subject to a genuine metamorphosis of their own, with the probable purpose of making us unrecognizable to the enemy. In this way our identity resides in our teeth, I thought, and I now confirm my belief in those conclusions.

To return to our dispute, once again I declined the offer of the dentist who, as I can say today, used all his forces of persuasion to make me agree to have my two teeth filed down and then crowned. As we all know, in the face of the terror we all feel in the face of disease and doctors, we become children again. So I let the dentist file down my two teeth and apply the gold crowns. From that moment, he began to demand from me something that I had never promised him. He tried to make me feel doubly guilty: for having neglected my teeth despite knowing that I was particularly susceptible to diseases of the oral cavity, and for not having absolved the debts I had contracted with him. For fear of his reproaches I hid, I avoided him, I erased him from my thoughts, but at the same time I made every effort to satisfy his requests. Fortunately my intentions were unsuccessful, or today I should have to reproach myself with having given encouragement to a charlatan. That, in fact, is what I consider him to be, because, after nine years, the dentist's professional inexperience has been fully revealed. The

recession of my gums revealed the faulty application of the
crowns, too open at the sides, allowing micro-organisms
into the dental pulp and leading to the formation of a granuloma and the extension of the infection to a good part of
the upper left semi-arch. At this point my scruples vanished:
if anyone is guilty, it is the man who attempted to corrupt
me with words and with gold. I should like to add the following: we are facing major imminent changes, and I am
sure that at the summit of Falzarego, like the marksman
chosen to shoot a lead bullet into the buttocks of that illustrious figure, and like so many unknown soldiers who have
risked their lives without any real benefit to themselves, we
have contributed to the creation of this new world.

In the wake of the attempted assassination, the victim's
prestige increased enormously, and he was able to become an
emissary in the great transformations of the political face of
our planet. Maestro G. was unjustly sentenced to three years'
imprisonment in his own country. Dr Taussig, on the other
hand, made no contribution to anything: his titanium
implants are systematically rejected by the body, whose minus-
cule antibodies possess a truly titanic force in the face of the
speculations of an irresponsible dentist. Because of him my
two teeth, loose by now, had to be extracted and thrown into
the rubbish bin. I wasn't even able to save the gold, repelled
by the idea that the imprint of my life would survive me, as I
had put it to Dr Taussig. I was also repelled by the idea that
the imprint of my life might be melted in a little oven, to be
placed in someone else's mouth, or to adorn a lady's wrist or
finger.

In the name of those ten agitated and confused years, in the name of all the teeth that fall out injustly, I ask compensation for the damage that Dr Taussig did to me.

NOTE: Dr Taussig was cleared, and I had to pay the costs of the trial. Rachel turned her back on me in bed every night for five years.

UL5

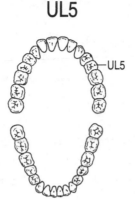

One day I found myself in Hong Kong negotiating the manufacture of dolls made according to our country's folk tradition. Emerging from a sampan, I felt a searing pain in the middle toe of my left foot. During the days that followed the pain grew, and I went in search of a doctor. I found Dr Mayer from Trieste, whose family originally came from my city. This intern, over fifty years of age, tall, bald, pock-marked, sent me to a little Chinese healer and reflexologist. Through this I discovered that the pain in my middle toe was really the reflex pain of some damage, which had until that point remained hidden, in my second upper left premolar.

'This toe corresponds to this tooth. Just trust, just trust. Go to dentist, have them take out this premolar, or treat it, and the toe stop hurting, you'll see,' said the Hong Kong reflexologist in his pidgin English.

He was right. After three days of searching I found Dr Baum, born in Paris but originally from Prague, who filled the caries in my tooth. UL5 was carious in its left lateral face, which meant that the caries was visible.

That day saw the death of an old revolutionary, president of China, the largest republic on earth. Perhaps it was at the very moment of his demise that I got up from Dr Baum's dentist's chair, noting with amazement that my middle toe had ceased to hurt. 'There are connections between the most remote parts of the body, and that applies to history, and to the universe. Is that coincidence?' I thought that morning. This idea inspired me for a further six years, giving me an insight into the fundamental principles of existence. Subsequently my life became entangled in lies, false and true emotions, and the light gradually went out. Since then I have been in a disagreeable penumbra, in which I seem to be half blind. Would totally blind not be better?

LL1

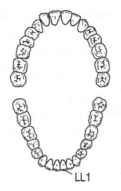

LL1

Second and final story of senile love

To my first lower left incisor I entrust my most intense and wretched love affair. Even today I cannot understand how such an obsession could lead a human being (and the male of the species in particular) to behave so unwisely, and to feel such absurd emotions and fantasies as those of a person in love. In addition, when this state arises in a person of about fifty years of age, the effects can threaten his very existence. If, today, I compare the story of LL1 with my own inexplicable, inexpressible love for a girl called Judith, I have various reasons for doing so. First of all because I have followed the fate of this incisor with particular attention, LL1 being in a sense the 'spy' upon the state of my whole being. Never having required any repairs or treatments of any kind, this tooth remained in place for more than sixty years, Nevertheless, it gradually blackened for no apparent reason, though it turned white again for some months after cleaning, and then, one fine day, quite by surprise, its blackening process recommenced. The phenomenon could not have been dependent on smoke because, many years after I stopped smoking, the tooth turned yellowish at the edges and brown at the centre. In the same way my spirit, during my acquaintance with Judith, always darkened again after short intervals of brightness. However much I tried to wear away that darkness (as I had with my tooth, using bicarbonate of soda) with extravagant statements of love and pathetic acts of apparent altruism, it returned inside me with irresistible obstinacy. Now that I may be about to confront the eternal darkness, I realize the extent to which my incisor, stupidly immobile in the middle of my jawbone, was the image of myself, stuck amidst other human beings in a petrified and threatening wood. We may become agitated, we may feel great despair or great happiness, but in reality we are always there, motionlessly nailed to life and to ourselves, and forever growing darker, forever darker.

The other reason why LL1 in some way constitutes the symbol of my story with Judith is that after the devastation of my teeth, which occurred during the final period of our stormy relationship, this incisor remained practically alone in the lower arch, resisting all dentures, bridges and other apparatuses ready to take its place. It was testimony of my irreducible attachment to everything and, in the end, of my loneliness. Then it went as well.

But there is a third reason that leads me to speak at such

length of that small, flat tenant of my oral cavity. The first black spot appeared on its vestibular face on the day when, in a far-off country in South America, a certain general decided to occupy the post of his nation's president, and assembled in a huge stadium thousands and thousands of people who then disappeared, either shot or tortured to death. Will this slaughter, which happens all around the world more and more frequently, be explained one day, or is it a condition assigned by fate to mankind?

But let us allow the facts to speak for themselves, in their own language. I met Judith one freezing March evening during a party at my country's embassy in Rome. On this occasion Maestro G. was supposed to meet up with some attachés from the Chinese embassy, although they didn't come to the meeting. The Maestro waited for an hour, then said his goodbyes to myself and the assembled company, and left the Renaissance palazzo, the seat of the cultural activities of our representatives. When I say cultural activities, what I have in mind is the more or less secret and more or less legal relations of every country's diplomatic corps. It is clear that the term sometimes covers the most abject behaviour of which human society is capable: plans for massacres, betrayals, the most hideous slaughter. Unfortunately I am now inclined to believe that the prophetic word 'culture' is more accurately applied to these outrages than to any great artistic masterpieces, or to the more unbelievable discoveries made by science. Such things are ingenious expressions of fine feelings and nothing more, merely demonstrating what man can do as a way of asserting his own superiority over his peers.

When I noticed her, Judith was leaning against a column

with a glass in her hand, looking at the assembled company. Her rich, thick black hair, hanging around her shoulders, her lips painted a lively red, her dark blue pleated skirt which didn't reach her knees, her fashionable little blue red-hemmed jacket, like an eighteenth-century *velada*, made me think of a character in a strip cartoon. Our eyes met at some point in mid-air. A moment later two fat guests came and stood between us. I walked around them. When I reached their shoulders, I found Judith was already halfway between where she had just been and where I was. We stopped, I looked around as though I just happened to be there, while she came towards me and started talking to me gently, in a hoarse, dark, whispering voice. 'I know you.'

'Could be,' I answered, so as not to close the door on a real acquaintance, but sure for my part that I had never met her before.

'We've seen each other in the community cafés,' she went on. It wasn't true, because I'd never been there even by mistake. But I repeated a 'could be', more forcefully this time, given that she was defining my possible membership of an ethnic-religious group. After a while we were joined by a very beautiful woman, tall, blonde and with a graceful bearing. The two women looked at each other; then Judith whispered a phrase to her, much as she had to me. 'We know each other.' The new arrival looked at her, smiled and pronounced the name that was later to be the torment of my clouded mind.

'Judith . . .'

'I saw you before, I was glancing over at you but you never saw me.'

'You were glancing over at me? Don't you remember my name? I'm Margarita.'

'I didn't remember. I just remembered your legs. No one could ever forget them.'

'You like my legs?'

Judith closed her big dark eyes and nodded her head, smiling.

A few moments later I learned that Margarita was a well-known ballerina at the city opera, and Judith a designer. Her whole world was contained in the shapes recorded in her mind, and within that world Margarita's legs danced with vivacious elegance. The mysterious conspiracy between the two girls unsettled me. I had never found myself in the presence of two girls bound by such a level of complicity. I looked from one to the other until I heard Judith whispering, 'Come on, let's go and get something to eat. Do you want me to serve you?'

At this point, in my mind, the image of Judith began to grow complicated in a way that was almost unbearable. An overwhelming curiosity led me to mouth the words, while we approached the big table with plates and food laid in rows. 'Can I come and see you one of these days?' I asked quietly.

'Of course,' she murmured with a smile. Her lips grew fuller when she smiled, unlike most people's.

That evening I couldn't take my eyes off her. She had the graceful figure of a little eighteenth-century soldier. Before the party was over I approached her again, scribbled her address on a little piece of paper and gave her mine. I didn't sleep at all that night. Judith's body and the ballerina's legs held sleep at bay. The next morning, the Maestro came to get me, bringing me the news of what had happened in that remote country in South America. 'You're not listening to me,' he said, seeing me disturbed and narcoleptic. 'And yet we're going to have to set off for Latin America any day.'

I thought about Rachel and the children, and was bitterly ashamed of the scant attention I paid them . . . That morning while shaving I noticed the dark veneer covering LL1. I wondered if the black might have been deposited on the surface of the tooth during the night, or if it had been there for months and years without my noticing. I decided to give my teeth a general clean, an exercise I had repeated so many times to no avail, and called Dr Fischer. My old compatriot carried out the work required five days later in his beautiful surgery at the top of the Gianicolo.

Secret events, not to be related even years later, took me far away. Let us say that I followed Maestro G. on his tour of Latin America and was rewarded with unforgettable nocturnal conversations. Not only did he reveal many of the secrets of contemporary music, he also shed light on the origins of my suffering, revealing the cause of many of the pains I had endured and the injustices committed against me. While he was waiting for assignations in the strangest places, he talked to me about the Latin and the Hebrew civilizations, and of the merits of the latter over the Anglo-Saxon and the Celtic; his mind seemed in supreme control. He spoke to me of Dionysus and the joyously chaotic life-force of the Mediterranean peoples; he talked of materialism and the Hegelian dialectic. His ardent faith in earthly justice and the human intellect dissolved, for a time, my inexplicable, desperate lack of faith in the goodness of life. I returned to my

homeland calmed and inspired, filled with the adolescent certainty that the quest for truth and a sense of goodness, let's call
it love for the human race, were enough to resolve all the
problems of existence. I loved Rachel and my children with a
new and freer emotion, and I was prepared to sacrifice myself
for them at any time.

'Are you sure you've changed that much?' Rachel asked me
one night. 'At a certain age you stop changing.'

'You change, you change,' I answered. I was sure I had
finally achieved self-realization, as they say these days.

I was transferred back to Rome. My family was to join me
two or three months later. I set off, and my fate was fixed.

My activity in the Italian capital required a great deal of
work, and I was only free in the evening. When there was no
embassy reception I went home – I was staying in a little
apartment belonging to our Cultural Institute – and waited
for orders and communications. One evening I felt the desire
to speak to someone, to meet a human being to whom I
could talk about something, and savour the warmth and the
sense of solidarity of which Maestro G. had so often spoken.
I flicked through my old diary – I had two, a secret one and a
public one. I don't need to say where I'd jotted down Judith's
number. My eye fell on it by chance. The curiosity I had felt
months previously returned, and after a moment's hesitation I
decided to call her. I knew nothing about her situation:
whether she was married, whether she was living with someone, what job she really did. I prepared my mind for a neutral
and hypocritical conversation. I got through to an answering
machine with Judith's voice. Immediately I recognized her
persuasive and mysterious tone, rather like a child confiding

secrets, a bit hoarse, almost masculine, which had struck me so much the only time I had talked to her. I said my name, specified the day and the time, but as to the reason for the call I couldn't think of anything, so I simply said: 'The reason . . . I don't know.' Immediately afterwards I felt ashamed, but it was too late by then. For three days no one responded. On the fourth day I found a short message in the porter's office at the Institute. 'The lady's been looking for you . . .' At the foot of the little piece of paper written in fountain pen was her name. 'If you can, at half past six the day after tomorrow be at the entrance to the Orangery. If you're busy we'll meet up some other time.'

It was the hour arranged for a meeting with our Foreign Minister, who was visiting Rome. At issue was my loyalty to the state, to the interests I represented and, more specifically, my own support for the ideal that had led me to accept my role and mission. On other occasions I would have sent everything and everyone to the devil just to be able to meet not just a minister, but the director of some minor state company. That day I felt terrible twinges in my chest, and the staff of the Institute, all engaged in making preparations for the reception, were worried, but in the end they let me go to the cardiologist on my own. At half past six that evening I turned up at the Orangery. The air was warm and balmy. After a short while, a little red car appeared in the square and Judith got out. Her slim, slender figure, her provocative curves, her flowing, rich black hair all impressed me more than they had the first time, all the more so since the girl – or rather the woman of about thirty – was wearing a very clinging white cotton dress with a pattern of little red and blue flowers. Her very

high heels gave her an almost dancing step. 'For what good
deed have I deserved such grace?' I wondered. But there,
already, was Judith's deep, velvety voice with a cheerful, con-
fidential 'Good evening'. I couldn't believe my eyes, my
emotions. 'This woman, so beautiful, so charming, is coming
to meet me of all people? How can that be? It must be some
kind of joke! She's making fun of me!' Doubts about my
character, about my diffident nature were about to poison
that first moment of happiness. But she held out a hand, took
me by the arm and together we passed through the illumi-
nated garden, embarking on our agitated, stormy adventure.

That evening she invited me to a friend's house and I didn't
leave until dawn. I was so happy, so brimful with her beauty
and loving grace, with my newly reborn capacity for the act of
love, that I didn't even stop to wonder why Judith hadn't
invited me to her house. I didn't want to know anything
about her, at least nothing more than she could have confided
herself. I knew that her father was Neapolitan and her mother
Jewish, from Ancona. Two souls coexisted within her, so that
Judith was everything I most ardently desired: the personifi-
cation of the great, chaotic freedom of the Mediterranean
people and, at the same time, of the most ascetic, the most
ancient severity. It was an encounter with everything I had
yearned for since my first classes in elementary school, during
my studies of philosophy and Marxism at university, during
the first years of my marriage. I will never forget those days
and nights of passion, so inexplicable, so invincible that it left
not the slightest space for any other thought or sensation.
Back then, I asked nothing, I wanted nothing from her. When
I went home to my own country for a week, and upon my

return found her with two huge bruises on her wrist and
ankle, I asked no questions, I felt no jealousy. I accepted her
for what she was, a creature free and light and at the same
time very profound and serious. Her voice was the same: one
moment it was slender and high, like a child's, the next it was
low, hoarse and almost masculine.

At the time I had not yet read the writings of a great student of the mind, born almost a hundred years ago in my
country, who had devoted a short pamphlet to the subject of
the 'double voice' in certain human beings. The mystery of
the voice remains one of the greatest for me. The voice comes
from the head, a kind of box of bone, and is propagated, via
the vibration of the air, to another bony box: someone else's
head. From this simple and inexplicable fact emerge wars,
religion, poetry, screams, weeping and laughter, revolutions,
despair, slaughter. Even within ourselves, within our consciousness, we hear it reverberating, although we can
remember it only for a few fractions of a second. The voices
of our loved ones, after their deaths, fall silent for ever: we can
hear them again in memory and dreams for a tiny fragment of
time. Otherwise, all that remains is the vacuous concept of the
low or high or hoarse or velvety voice. But these are, as I say,
merely concepts.

During the week I spent in my homeland I made enormous efforts to confide to Rachel what was going on in my
mind. She looked at me, her eyes blank, and said: 'Our children . . . What's going to happen to them?'

'I don't know,' I answered. 'But I feel I have to go through
this experience. I couldn't fight it. For the good of us all, I
have to go my own way.'

Rachel, my mild, solid, indestructible Rachel, looked at me, went to say goodnight to the children and then went to bed. It may be that in her sleep she sought the advice of the Eternal One, who took her with him, because till dawn, till the hour of my departure, she remained motionless, as though all life had left her. At five o'clock she got up, put on her wretched, threadbare dressing gown and made me my morning coffee. Inside that horrendous blue wool wrapping I imagined her warm, maternal body, the one I was fleeing from. I tried to call Italy from the airport. It was six o'clock in the morning. I got the usual hoarse and confiding voice of the answering machine. Where could she be at that time of day? I didn't wonder any more, I had no right to. I was married, and I had just got out of the bed that I had, for a week, shared with Rachel.

When I arrived, I found Judith waiting for me. She had remembered everything; after an interval of eight days she knew the precise time of my arrival and the flight number. We embraced and she took me to her friend's house. For three hours that morning our bodies rocked with passion, and Judith's groans now low and masculine, now high and virginal, irresistibly roused me to new pitches of erotic intensity.

'I've missed you so much,' she murmured as she dressed.

'Did you ever think of me?' I asked.

'Always. And I always imagined you the way you are with me. I couldn't think about anything else. But the thought that you might be with your wife was terrible to me.'

'You're not one of those girls who stay single just to destroy other people's marriages?' I asked, once again trying desperately to save my family.

'How ridiculous!' she exclaimed. 'You're talking about the
will to destruction. No, nothing like that. I'm faithful, honest,
absolutely honest. You'll never understand. The mere thought
that you might be constantly lying, to me and your wife,
makes me feel quite ill. I'd rather not see you again. Come
back when you're free.'

I told her I'd spoken to Rachel, that in some remote corner
of my being the lie was still the worst, the most terrible thing
that could infect humanity.

She smiled. 'There are worse things. You don't have to say
everything. You just have to admit certain little lies. The worst
thing is to take away someone's freedom. In a sense, by spending some time with your wife, some time with me, you are
taking my freedom away. You're taking away my freedom to
be alone, to experience that passion with you.'

She walked me to the Institute and for five days, although
I looked for her everywhere, leaving messages on her answering machine every half-hour, I was unable to find her. My
days began to fill with constant and futile attempts to track her
down. In the evening, when my work was over, I walked
beneath the windows of the house she had taken me to on a
number of occasions, and waited hour after hour in the hope
that she might suddenly appear. It never occurred to me to
look for her at her house. For me, that place didn't exist, I had
never been invited there, and when I went to collect her
Judith was always waiting for me by the door. I had never
wondered about this: clearly I was afraid of entering that kind
of sanctuary that she kept hidden from me, as if the scrolls of
the law were preserved there.

On the fifth day of her absence, there was an engaged tone

on her line. Either she was at home, talking feverishly and at
length to someone, or she had taken the receiver off the hook
so she could be at home without being disturbed. For the first
time since I had known her, images of Judith in thrall to some
headless male body flashed before my eyes. I banished those
images with all my strength, but they came back for a second,
or for minutes at a stretch. I was losing my mind. After ten
days or so, with a feeling of unbearable emptiness, when I was
beginning to give up the idea of ever finding the woman
who had appeared centre stage in my life, Judith's line suddenly became free again. I called her for three hours, uselessly
and repeatedly pressing the square keys corresponding to the
eight digits of her number. No one replied. Finally, at about
midnight, I heard her usual voice, mysterious and exciting:
Judith in person!

   'How are you? You've been out of touch for so long!' she
said, greeting me with joy and surprise. I started stammering
like a schoolboy. For a second I didn't notice the absurdity of
what Judith was saying. I'd been out of touch? Hadn't it been
she who was hiding, who had disappeared? I didn't want to
think about it. I felt like a new man, a youth embarking on his
love life, a novice full of hope. Judith arranged a time to meet
up for the following day and I started counting the hours.
Family, work, ideals, everything had vanished from my horizon. All that remained was the thought of Judith. Never with
such clarity had I been aware of the difference between 'I' and
'you' (and 'she' in my interior monologues), but I didn't
understand the degree to which I was chaining myself to
Judith, how much could be put down to my obsessive tendencies, how dependent on her I was. I was tempted to

identify her as the source of all my uncertainties and delights as the woman who had, for the first time in my life, made me feel that emotion that the French call *amour passion*. All of a sudden, looking at myself in the mirror the morning of the following day, I noticed the brown stain on the vestibular surface of LL1. 'How am I going to show myself to her with that terrible incisor?' a voice screamed inside me which, in this instance, remained sealed in the box that was my head, or in my heart or, in the abstract, if we wish to believe in the 'mind', in my very being. Once again I needed to see Dr Fischer, but he was on holiday in Sicily and wasn't going to be back for another three weeks. I began brushing the lower dental arch furiously. The incisor, positioned between LL2 and LR1, and slightly set back from them, would not be cleaned. Resolving to go to any dentist at all, I started flicking through the telephone directory, then grew frightened, and thus LL1 ended up completely blackened.

That morning I learned from Maestro G. that the people's republics of a great Asian state were about to dissolve their union, and that they were on the point of declaring war on each other. Right in the middle of the elegant Café Greco, Maestro G. started to weep tears akin to those that I, some months later, would weep over my unhappy love affair. He was weeping for something which went beyond emotion, which had something to do with ideals.

'How can you weep for an ideal?' I wondered, and the Maestro, wiping away his tears, said: 'I have never wept for a human being. When my father died, when my wife gave birth to a lifeless child, I stayed dry-eyed, but now I can't hold back the tears. I'm in despair. Two brother countries, with the same goals and the same traditions, declaring war on each other!' What did his despair consist of? What was the thread of his pain attached to? To an ideal? Back then I felt great admiration for the Maestro, who now arouses in me only a vague sense of pity, and sometimes of anger and contempt.

On that occasion I thought I understood the pain of the mind. With Judith I was to discover another, more terrible pain: that of the emotions. I saw her again that day, and my love returned, renewed. I became aware of the charm of her elusive character a thousand times while we were embracing, she appeared before my closed eyes, in the strangest and most exciting postures. Did I love her, or did I love what I imagined when I was with her? Conversely, I really didn't love her evasive answers.

'You want to know why so many days passed and who I was with? But why don't you ask yourself where you were?'

'I was here, waiting for you,' I answered.

'But before that you were with your wife,' Judith insisted. 'You impose your conditions on me. I was with my brother who had just come back from Brazil to see me. While you were in bed with your wife.'

A few months later I learned that Judith had no brothers. Why did she lie like that? Who was she hiding, who was she protecting? At that time in my life I had already discovered the value of sincerity (see p. 194). My past, the difficulties of my private life had taught me that sincerity was the basis of every correct human relation, of social life, of life itself. For Judith the basis of all of these things was freedom.

Despite my doubts and worries about my tooth, and the political transformations underway throughout the world, during those weeks we met very often, always at her friend's house. One day I was called to the ambassador who, after two minutes of abrupt discussion, handed me an envelope. 'This will be the usual official communication about holidays,' I thought, but hardly had I caught sight of the letter typed on double-lined paper, than I recognized the style of the person who had been guiding my actions for ten years now: Maestro G. His letter contained words of censure and vague, not excessively frightening threats. I realized that during those recent months I had neglected my mission. It had admittedly required lengthy periods of waiting and idleness, and for that reason I didn't feel too guilty. But worse than those reproaches was what happened shortly afterwards: Rachel arrived with the children. I thought I was finished. Everything I had wished for in my life – love, childish tenderness, appeasement of the erotic instincts – was there within my reach, in the mysterious and graceful person of Judith. Now all that was to come to an end in an instant, making way for my duty, by now antiquated and hardly tenable, as head of the family. But what if that role had passed entirely to the state? No, I mustn't yield. And I didn't yield.

The day she arrived in Rome I decided to talk to Rachel. I felt like the prisoner sent to Siberia for punishment who, having to urinate at thirty degrees below zero, was obliged to expel needles of ice from his bladder. Words and the truth that they express have always had that devastating effect on me anyway. That evening I told Rachel, who was mortally wounded by my every syllable, everything I could about my 'relationship' with Judith.

'We've discussed it before,' my wife said finally. 'I know everything and I accept everything.'

'But I don't,' I replied. 'I have to live day and night with the person you know about; you can't prevent me from taking that experience to its conclusion. That way everything will be over very soon. She doesn't care, she's got someone else. And now let me go to her.' I put on my old winter coat, typical of the inhabitants of eastern Europe. Rachel locked the door and blocked my way.

'You're staying here,' she whispered.

I found myself in an impossible situation. Was I to get to my assignation with Judith and tell her I was free now, or was I to stay at home and resign myself to losing the object of my passion?

'Let me out,' I begged Rachel. 'It's pointless, I can't go back. Why do you want to start a scandal, here in the Institute? Do you want them to hear us screaming and cursing?'

'Yes!' she answered. 'I'm not letting you go. I'm not moving an inch.'

It was a tragic and ridiculous situation. The passing of the minutes taunted me. For the first time I felt the poisonous ticking of the seconds, the grotesque brevity, the unbearable length of life.

Rachel sat down. I was having trouble breathing and, shaken by a tremendous rage, I wanted to break everything fragile in the room, to hurl myself with my fists against the wooden door, massive, thick, dark and truly closed. Anything more closed than that I couldn't imagine in the universe.

But the bathroom door was open. I started slamming it,

opening it, slamming it again with all my strength, making a deafening crash. At this point, Rachel took the key from the pocket of her bathrobe and held it out to me, hissing between her teeth the most terrifying words that I had ever heard. 'You will be cursed for what you're doing to me and the children. Everything is going to go badly for you. You will be pursued by the blackest of curses for ever. You don't cause pain like that to the mother of your own children. You will be cursed in them as well. Never show your face to me again. Never!'

It was all over. I had to leave that miserable little room, like being expelled from paradise. I didn't know how to make my exit. In the face of those words, any gesture struck me as too normal, too ordinary. I went: as light as if I was made of air, rarefied beneath the weight of my banality.

Just then the incredible weakness in the lamellae of my jawbone returned. As if my whole defence in the face of the world had diminished, over a few weeks the bony part of my gums receded. I noticed that UL7 was wobbling in my mouth, like a ripe fruit wanting to drop from the branch. I would have left it as it was for another two years: I wasn't resigning myself to the idea of losing that gold-lined tooth. Besides, when chewing, every now and again an imprudent bite would give me a searing pain, but one that wasn't in the slightest sense unpleasant. That pain recalled me to myself, despite the confusion that dispatched me into a kind of eternal fog, with no awareness of myself or of my place in the world. LL1 began to grow inordinately black: I was forced to go to Dr Fischer, on the Gianicolo, to have it cleaned along with the rest of my teeth.

I had no homeland – I couldn't and wouldn't go home – no family, no work. I went to Judith and told her I was free, that she had me at her disposal. I told her about the terrible quarrel and its painful consequences. 'Be brave,' she said to me. 'If you like you can come and live at my place. What we have is true love.'

I accepted the invitation not suspecting the dangers that lay in wait for me. On a number of occasions during the months that followed I risked losing my last vestiges of sanity. In a sense it would have been better if I had because then I wouldn't have been aware of the abject depths of which a desperate man is capable.

Four months later Judith allowed me to set foot in her apartment for the first time. She did so without the solemnity due to the event, but with an indifferent lightness. 'Will you have dinner with me?' she asked, as if it was merely a social occasion. 'If it's OK with you, we can eat something at my place.'

She lived in a large *fin de siècle* block. A few yards away there rose the most famous dome in the world. We climbed to the fourth floor. Judith took out a heavy bunch of keys, chose two with some difficulty, opened first with one, then with the other. We entered her lair.

I immediately noticed the white walls, free of any decoration. There was practically nothing else to be seen, because of the great accumulation of cardboard boxes piled up in every room.

'Don't say a word about the untidiness. I've been living like this for two years. Since I got divorced,' said Judith. 'I've never had the courage to unpack these boxes. They contain all of my previous life.'

She lived barricaded in her new house, which held the ruins of the old one. I liked that meticulous chaos, which relieved me of all responsibility to be orderly or careful. I felt completely free. We dined by candlelight, and once again we fell into an erotic battle of tenderness and violence. I had returned to a primordial state. I could think only of our embraces.

Over the months that followed, while I waited for everything to be clarified and develop in the best way possible, I found a job as a night porter in a hotel not far from Judith's apartment. After so much studying, so many different jobs, so much wandering around the world, I gladly adapted to this truly unsuitable employment. The emotion meant nothing to me. What filled me with alarm was my distance from Judith during the very hours we could have spent in bed, embracing and making love as we had in the first months of our acquaintance. At first I phoned her every hour to check that she was alone, and she would answer with a shriek of joy that told me how much she loved me. When I went home at dawn, she made me a coffee and kissed me in a way that immediately reawakened my tired senses. In bed she pressed herself to me, and we made love until we were close to madness, without shame or inhibitions about any part of our respective bodies.

'I've never been so free,' Judith said to me. 'With your eastern passion, you've given me back my life.'

She told me about her divorce, her husband's betrayals, her own rigid morality and her playful, childish nature. I was very proud and reassured myself that I had found that twin spirit, that grain of corn which, as Tolstoy so expressively put it, had been marked along with another, before being thrown on to a wagon full of grain.

One night I called Judith for no reason. There was no reply. I tried again every half-hour, without success. Suddenly my jealousy reawakened. In my mind I pictured a sequence of scenes of unbridled lust between Judith and male strangers – a repertoire of pornography at its most banal and trite played out in my mind. When I got home, I found her in bed, calmly asleep.

'Why didn't you answer?' I screamed like a madman.

She stretched and asked, in the drawling voice of someone who can't quite free herself from sleep, 'What are you talking about? I haven't heard it ring since yesterday evening. You never called.'

I swore I had, dozens of times, all night long. Judith became angry. 'Your madness confuses reality and lies. Go to a psychiatrist if you've got problems like that.' She used words of surprising vulgarity. What had happened to sweet Judith, the sacrificial lamb of so many amorous battles, the dear creature with the child's voice? A hoarse, grave voice was now speaking from the cranial box of some unknown, unapproachable creature. I realized I was totally ignorant about her. I asked her forgiveness and lay down beside her body, not daring to move. For some days, Judith wouldn't let me touch her, declaring that the invitation to stay at her house had been cancelled by my actions. I saw myself lost. 'Am I doomed to wander the earth like Cain?' I wondered. I felt the most forlorn being in the world.

LL1 was getting blacker and blacker: during those months I was devoting very little attention to my oral hygiene. As I

said before, UL7 was also rocking increasingly in its left corner
at the back. I had invented a game that I never tired of repeating during the nocturnal hours at work: I pushed UL7 back
with my thumb, and then with the tip of my tongue I leaned
it in the opposite direction. I would do this for half an hour at
a stretch while I read the newspaper or tried to solve the
crossword in some magazine or other. I had lost all interest in
everything: all I could think of was Judith and me. At times,
when I was chewing, I would push mouthfuls of food beneath
the penultimate left upper molar, UL7, to feel the pain of
biting and experience the sudden vision of my tooth bending,
freeing itself from the ligaments and coming away from the
bone, bloody and broken. It was the fantasy of a self-mutilator,
as I well knew, but I was starting to suspect that my whole
existence bore the imprint of that irresistible and mysterious
impulse. 'Are we hurled into life so that we can damage ourselves? What sort of sick joke is this? Must we become our
own executioners so that the inventor of life can be absolved
from such misdeeds?'

One morning I went to Dr Fischer, told him about the
changes that had occurred in my life, and asked him to examine the state of my teeth, specially UL7 and LL1. Fischer
prescribed me an X-ray to be carried out in a different surgery
and wrote a note of recommendation to this end. The X-ray
revealed that UL7, no longer fixed in the maxilla, was now
hanging only from its ligaments. As to LL1, its colour might
be due to the presence of a fungus in my mouth. It was difficult to suggest other reasons, since I wasn't suffering from a
lack of calcium or iron.

That evening I spoke to Judith, who tried to dissuade me

from having anything done. 'Are you mad? Are you going to have them take out a tooth that won't grow back? Do you want to throw away a part of yourself? Consult other dentists, you'll see, they'll come up with something.'

I couldn't believe I was being encouraged to reject the dentist's intervention. I went on playing with UL7, pushing it back and forth, causing myself the subtle pleasure of pain. I brushed LL1 more and more vigorously to take away the blackness that came straight from my soul and wouldn't disappear.

By day, Judith designed and oversaw the page layout of a women's magazine. At dinner time I went to pick her up, to stop her coming out with the usual lies. Sometimes she had tried to persuade me that she had gone to dinner with friends and colleagues, when she had really disappeared for four or five hours. If I pointed this out to her, she reproached me severely, saying that my suspicions would be the cause of our separation. We were making love less frequently, and I noticed kinds of behaviour that had never been part of our erotic vocabulary. 'Who taught you to do that?' I asked her, and she would immediately break away and say, in words both tearful and angry, that I had ruined everything and that one day there would be no turning back, that we would have to part.

When I came home one morning I found she wasn't there. My heart started thumping: there we are, now you're going to have to tell me the truth, now I've caught you out, I thought. She came home half an hour later. The picture of innocence, she said she had spent the night with her sister, another designer. Some months later I learned that at this time the sister, who connived with her in everything, had been living in Brazil for some time. The women supported each other in their lies and mystification. Not a day went by without my deciding to pack my bags and go, although I didn't know exactly where, and each day when I met her, the desire for her love grew stronger in me.

The great political changes that had occurred in my country removed my hope of ever returning to my former work. Once again, the part of Europe that I came from threatened to become the centre of bloody clashes between races of people who had arrived in those lands a thousand years ago. It all caused me pain, but it didn't really worry me. I had a sense that the fate of the world had to be resolved between Judith and myself, that truth and lies had to fight it out in our minds and our bodies.

One night I did something I should never have done. Having left the hotel, locking the door behind me, I ran to Judith's apartment without warning her. She wasn't there. Convinced now that I had seen through all her lies, I was filled with a sense of triumph. 'It's not so easy to change the truth, to obscure it with your cleverness. The human mind can still reveal it,' I thought with bitter enthusiasm. I felt exaltation and pain at the same time and a terrible anguish constricted my chest. I turned on my heels, running at a breakneck pace. Outside the hotel three furious guests were waiting to be let in. I invented some pious excuse – my father had had a heart attack – and managed to smooth things over. In pursuit of the truth, I allowed the lies to accumulate.

In the morning I went back home and found Judith sleeping in her bed. 'This is her reward for all her phoney love-making. Her face is serene, she's sleeping like an animal!'

I thought, looking at her. 'I've got to free myself from this slavery.'

But before I allowed her guilt to crush me, I didn't dare sacrifice what I still had: the most intense, the most satisfying love of my life. Judith and I were in a position to make each other happy for life, even if I had to pay for every moment of happiness with unbearable suspicion, fear and agony. I felt she was lying to me, but I hadn't the means to discover with whom, where and why she was betraying me, since she kept me by her in spite of everything. The greater the effort I made to discover all her subterfuges, the darker LL1 became, and the more UL7 moved in its socket.

Fortunately the new government, which required my services, gave me some money and some minor tasks. In addition, certain foreign friends had managed to find me, and asked me favours from time to time. The moment I had a little money I bought jewels, shoes and clothes for Judith.

'Not even the most generous of my boyfriends has ever given me so many presents. You're the nicest man on earth,' she said. She was filled with gratitude if people paid her the slightest attention. She had started making love at the age of fourteen, at a time of revolution and deceptive changes. (I don't know how you escape the fatal illusion of progress: all I can see today is bloody slaughter, an eternal abattoir, outside time or history.)

Judith's amorous career had ended tragically on more than one occasion: one of her fiancés, a young architect belonging to the same political movement as she did, had died in her arms in a street incident, and the one who had taken his place, an engineer's son who had run away from home and made his living as a gambler, had died of a heart attack at the age of thirty.

'I, who so love life, have had to bury two fiancés,' Judith said every now and again.

'It's chance, the bloody game of chance,' I would say in an attempt to console her, and she would cover me with kisses and caresses.

'I don't regret a thing, if I can give so much happiness today, if I'm a little corrupt and a little innocent then I owe it to the men I have loved. Even two or three at the same time. Some of them knew of the others, some didn't. I've always made them all happy, they've all retained their affection for me,' said Judith, concluding the story of her life.

I started to become aware of a terrible danger. 'She wants to kill me as well,' I thought. Every time we kissed I had a sense I was suffocating, I felt as though my heart couldn't withstand this emotion for very long. Yet despite the terror of death, the moment Judith's soft and fluid body lay down beside me I was filled with an irresistible excitement. 'I'll die if I go on like this,' I repeated to myself, but each evening, every time I woke up, I sought Judith, her skin, the curves of her body.

'I've got to go to an exhibition opening this evening,' she said one day, just after we had woken up. 'When it's over I'll come and say hello at the hotel.' Around midnight I was sure she wasn't coming. Once again I left my post and went to her apartment. I crossed the courtyard with my heart in my mouth. The windows were in darkness. From behind the door I didn't know whether I would shortly hear Judith's cries of pleasure as she clung to some man, or whether, as was often the case, she would already be asleep. I opened the door, trying not to make the slightest sound. I went in. After a moment I realized that the house was empty. I turned on the light and went into the bedroom. Judith's clothes were scattered around the floor. She had changed and gone out in a hurry. I touched her damp sheets. I felt like crying, never had I been so degraded, never had I descended so deeply into the dark depths of pleasure. I stayed like that for a moment, then I ran to the hotel. Judith was waiting for me by the door. I screamed furiously at her and she, in a little child's voice, said, 'But what have I done wrong? Come here and give me a kiss.' She opened her arms, pressed me to her breast, made me feel her hot breath on my throat, the back of my neck, my ears. 'Don't be so hasty. You don't know anything about me. Don't let yourself get carried away.' She climbed into her little car and disappeared into the night. In the morning, the minute I got home, I slipped into bed where we made love until midday.

That evening, just before I went to work, I heard the entry-phone ringing. Judith said quickly: 'Don't open the door.'

'Why?'

'It's my sister, hopeless creature, sending a friend of hers to see me. I don't want to let him in.'

I went to the window to see who it was. Judith came over to me, embraced me and kissed me on the eyes. 'Only a trai-tor thinks constantly of betrayal,' she said with a laugh. The entryphone rang again. She picked up the receiver. 'Go and speak to my sister, she'll tell you everything!' she said in a forced tone, like someone talking to a deaf person, or some-one to whom they are trying to give a coded message. The visitor vanished into the darkness before I could see him.

The same kind of incident took place on two further occasions, and Judith constantly tried to reassure me, talking
now about the tax man, now about some importunate friend,
now about beggars. I didn't believe her. Will I have to repent
of such incredulity on the Day of Judgement, when the truth
becomes apparent, or will I have the bitter joy of seeing my
suspicions confirmed? Unable to bear the idea that my whole
life might have been focused on something so uncertain, I
resorted to a devious strategy. After saving a month's salary, I
hired a private investigator. I brought him some photographs
of Judith and talked to him about the two of us. In the apartment of this man, this employee of suspicion, I felt quite at
ease. I too had been through such a long phase of suspicions
and hidden plots: now I was reproducing those plots on a
smaller scale. Dr Falconi promised me the greatest discretion
and a definite outcome to the investigations. He took everything I possessed: I had really reached a nadir. I should have
had LL1, by now completely black, cleaned again; I should
have had UL7, which now moved and almost dangled freely
in my mouth, extracted, and instead I was spending my
money on the investigation of an impossible certainty.
Certainty and truth are the opposite of existence, and that
opposite was where I wanted to dwell. After a week I phoned
the investigator, and he confirmed what I had suspected for
some time: Judith had a lover. He gave me the man's address,
described his appearance, told me he had waited outside the
door from ten in the evening until two in the morning until
he saw Judith coming out, her manner unambiguous on this
boy's arm. Now I was really happy; finally my suffering was at
an end. I could go back to Rachel and the children, repent

everything and forget my tormentor for ever. I would find a job — after all I had two doctorates — I would lead a quiet life in my little nation, away from the powerful currents of history and the emotions. On a piece of paper I jotted down a memo about how I would behave with Judith, what words, what phrases I would say to her, what actions I would perform once I had secretly entered the house of my suffering, the luminous and chaotic apartment of the woman I loved in all the noble and ignoble variations of the meaning of that ancient word.

It all happened quite differently from what I had imagined. Judith's bed, neat and tidy, had only just been abandoned, that much was apparent to the touch. There was no trace in the house of lovers or other visitors. 'She's slept somewhere all night, then she's come back home for a moment to make it look as though she hasn't moved,' I thought, and a sort of impotent rage rose from my stomach to my heart, and from there to my head. I was filled to the brim with anguish and excitement. During those minutes I really felt as if I might burst, so great was this sense of fullness.

I looked around, thought for a moment of setting fire to the apartment, and then resolved to smash to pieces all the windows, the wash-basin, the chairs, everything it was in my power to destroy. 'Calm down, calm down, I beg you,' said the more tranquil part of my mind. I sat down and breathed deeply. Gradually the rage transformed into infinite self-pity, I started to weep. I gathered together everything I could, jumbled it all together into an old suitcase and went down the stairs. 'Where shall I go?' I wondered, after leaving the house keys in the letterbox along with a miserable note of farewell.

I was really alone in the world, I was like someone escaping slavery in Egypt. Ahead of me was a desert, in which I could wander for forty years if I had that long to live. I couldn't go home again. I stood by the door until five in the afternoon, when Judith came home from her usual trip around the news-paper offices. She promised each editor a few hours of pleasure: she did so with discretion, with only a look or a fleeting allusion. But in all likelihood she ended up granting them more than they might have hoped. Her lips were smeared with red as though she had been kissing passionately and for a long time. She was clearly convinced that there was nothing to be seen.

'How are you?' she asked me, quite naturally. She didn't seem especially keen to see me, but seeing me with my suit-case she started laughing and invited me to come back up, if only for a coffee. 'Why does she want me back in her apart-ment?' I wondered, unable to find an answer.

I went back to my house of suffering, amongst the piled-up cardboard boxes, and of course, a few minutes later, I was in Judith's bed. During the night I woke up three or four times and started looking at the face of the woman sleeping beside me. 'A pile of flesh that will dissolve in a few weeks, all of this. A machine that works for a few decades with pre-arranged movements, and is then thrown away,' I thought. I too must appear more or less the same: a pitiful collection of proteins, a useless and stupid mechanism. After all these years I thought of suicide. For a moment I saw my head crashing against the asphalt, I heard the terrible impact after my fall. 'No, I mustn't set my children an example like that!' echoed the voice in the flux of my consciousness. In fact, some alarm signal must have gone off in my brain, some connection of neurones devoted to the instinct of self-preservation.

I got up and went to the bathroom. I turned on the light and in the mirror, set in an astonished and bovinely stupid face, I stared at a row of white teeth, more or less dilapidated, holed and patched, and in the middle a black incisor a little longer than its neighbours, rising like a solitary horseman against the sunset. At that very moment, I felt UL7 wobbling as I pushed it with my tongue. The subtle pleasure that came from that dangling tooth brought to mind the petty problems of my body and my constant and minute attention in studying it, anticipating the final disaster. Focusing on the pain of UL7 I suddenly became aware that all my teeth were hurting, that my whole mouth was in pain.

'Where are you?' echoed Judith's sleepy voice. 'Come here, next to me. Why do you always run away?' What did she expect from a wreck like me? Did she have no other instrument for her pleasure? 'Come here so I can caress you!' I locked the bathroom door so as not to be close to Judith, now that I had found my reason to stay alive: the relationship between my teeth. As I had been chewing with the right-hand side for months and months, because of the terminal condition of UL7, the left-hand side had weakened, and the bone that holds the teeth was about to rupture as well. If I wanted to save myself, I would have to cut Judith from the centre of my being, extract her from me. If I had UL7 extracted, perhaps LL1 would stop going black, perhaps my soul would not darken. The two facts seemed absolutely independent of each other, but I was convinced of the contrary. I spent a few hours crouched in the bathroom thinking about what to do next.

'I'll be back at five, if you want the keys, I'll leave them on the table. You decide. If you're here when I get back, let's stay together, otherwise . . . goodbye.' From behind the closed door of the bathroom I heard the apartment door click shut. Judith had gone out to attend to her business. I had to decide how to get rid of her, or whatever part of me she represented. I stayed.

For months I spent my days spying on her, following her in the street, trying to guess who her lovers were. At the end of this thankless and fruitless daytime occupation, I returned to my job as a night porter. I stretched out on a sofa in the hall of the hotel, and my mind projected the figure of Judith into the darkness: I saw her with her lovers, I heard her unequivocal whispers. 'I've got to free myself from her,' I said to myself. As I couldn't decide to act on this resolution and I immediately yielded to the first caresses of this phantom, I tried to think up various strategies to buttress my resolve. I began to address myself, in my internal discourses, in the second person singular. 'You've got to pay attention!' I admonished myself. Or else I tried to give myself peremptory commands: 'Leave this house!' After a few weeks everything had turned into these commands and my corresponding disobedience. It was a ludicrous kind of see-saw, which I soon abandoned.

One evening Judith came home and ordered me to polish her shoes. 'I'm not your slave!' I exclaimed, and she started laughing.

'A simple act of kindness and you see it as slavery. My

husband often used to polish my shoes, and I often polished his. That's how it is with people who love each other.'

With furious diligence I polished her little leather shoes. She got dressed up and went out for a work dinner. 'I'll come with you!' I said, in the dull voice of a jealous man trying to preserve his own dignity.

'No, I'm going to dinner with some old friends, we'll only be talking about work!' said Judith, in such a false and uncertain tone that it was perfectly clear what she was going to do. That woman, fundamentally incapable of lying, actually did it all the time. 'Does she realize it or not?' I asked myself.

Strangely, if I didn't believe her she grew angry. Her rage, again, was a clue to her sincerity. When I didn't believe her about something that was plainly true, she didn't actually get angry, but when she lied without being believed, all her fury was roused as if she had to defend a sacred truth. That day, too, she answered irritably. 'It's nothing serious. What do those people have to do with you?'

'But I'm your . . .'

'My what?' Judith asked in a challenging tone. She had made me give up everything that was important to me and now she was humiliating me, mocking me. In that moment the only thing I could think of was to raise my hand and slap her with all my strength. Judith came closer to me. 'Don't do anything you'll regret a moment later!' My mind, my muscles were invaded by impulses I could not keep in check, I felt savage forces rising up in me, as if I were a wild animal. I took her neck between my hands and began to press. 'Careful, you may regret this in a moment,' Judith said coldly.

'Isn't she worried about dying? Can she only think of my

repentance?' I pondered as I let go of her. Immediately she moved away, hissing between her teeth: 'Go!'

She had been right: I already regretted hurting her. But this time she screamed with all the breath she had in her body: 'Go away from here! And never let me see you again! You're an animal!'

Once I had gathered together all the things I had brought to that lovely, disordered apartment, I went away, feeling a sense of shame and defeat. I had touched rock bottom, now I really had no one, I was no one. At the hotel where I worked, I asked the manager if I could stay a few days in a lumber-room I had noticed a while previously. At seven in the morning, once my shift was over, I locked myself in there. Lying on a folding camp bed, I tried to think about my life, my future. Strangely, I didn't feel anxious. I woke up at midday. I went to the kitchen and asked them to make me a good hot coffee. I felt light, carefree as a schoolboy. Perhaps throughout my whole life I had been looking for that state of total suspension, of nullity. Identity was too heavy for me, I wanted to throw it out, to allow myself to dissolve in an existence without sense or meaning.

The manager handed me a letter that had just arrived. On the envelope I recognized Rachel's handwriting.

'We're still here, your children and me. The family hasn't been torn apart, there hasn't been a divorce, either here or in any other country. Come and see us and don't think that you have been relieved of your responsibilities just because you're in despair. Apart from that, I love you and you won't be granted a remission on that so easily either. We're waiting for you. Your grandchildren are always asking after you.

"Grandad's in love," we tell everyone, Leah first. "In love? What's that? Does it mean we can't see him?" Samuel is a very ugly but very intelligent boy. May the Eternal One preserve you. Yours, Rachel.'

At that moment I had an impulse to return to Rachel and my children (and grandchildren). I wanted to go and get my railway ticket straight away, and was about to go and see my colleague in the porter's lodge to ask his help. Just then, through the glass-panelled door, I saw a slender figure, wrapped in a black coat, with dark, gleaming hair piled up in a little chignon, face hidden by big dark glasses and shoulders covered by a black scarf. A figure ludicrously redolent of fate, but at the same time one that was somehow benevolent, domestic. It was Judith, who had come to look for me, to bring me back to her lair. For her the universe was something confused but homogeneous, and she didn't want to undermine that homogeneity with her own actions.

So I went back to Judith's once again. 'But what about you, why do you want me to stay with you?' I asked one evening.

'I don't know,' she answered candidly. Then she added some unexpected reflections. 'I'm not a child any more, I've looked around and I haven't found any free men who interest me. You've interested me so far. You're completely outside any social classification, you're above any possible classification. And then I think that over all those years, with all the things you've got up to around the world, you must have stashed a fair bit away somewhere or other.'

So Judith thought, deep down, that I was something of a catch! Me, the most derelict being, the most socially unclassifiable, the most uncertain, with the least esteem for himself and whoever it was who had hurled him into existence! So she was gullible, the poor girl, far from being astute and clever! I felt a sense of enormous pity for her, a truly profound emotion, that might even have been considered an impulse of love, while in reality it was nothing but that famous compassion that the Judaeo-Buddhist Schopenhauer describes as the only possible feeling we can have towards another human being.

From that moment onwards, my jealousy started to decline. On the other hand my desire to live up to the model that Judith, in her innocence, had assigned to me, began to increase. Each evening I ordered sumptuous bouquets of flowers – mostly lilies – to send to her apartment; I gave her all kinds of presents, shoes, purses, blouses, getting through my entire salary in this way. At the hotel, in any case, I always found something to eat, and I had no other requirements. I thought my lifestyle during those months, that year and a half, was excellent. I was perfectly camouflaged by the most complete mediocrity, fate couldn't get me in its clutches in any way, I had reduced my needs, every aspect of my life, to zero.

During those weeks, fifty years on, another war had broken out in Europe. One federal state had suddenly divided into many little statelets, all of them proud of their own ethnic purity, and resolved to defend it with the most modern armies and the most ancient ferocity. An undercover traffic in destruction had grown up around that war. Old friends and enemies started seeking me out again. Curiously, with the outbreak of that insane conflict, my mouth became inflamed as well. In the roots of UL7, the abscess Dr Fischer had warned me about began to form, and LL1 also began to give me pain after I brushed my teeth in the evening. I showed my swollen mouth to nocturnal visitors who tried to involve me in new missions. 'When this has stopped giving me agony I'll give you an answer,' I would repeat. One of those who had come to find me was Maestro G., in even greater despair than before.

'I don't conduct concerts any more, music has no meaning for me without the central idea of man's destiny on earth. In any case, I don't have any particular talent. I was attached to the idea of solidarity between the poor that was called "dialectical materialism" for the very reason that I'm not very talented.'

He went off into the night and I never saw him again: the darkness of time had dissolved for me. This master of life, this man I had adored and venerated, had simply disappeared off the horizon.

Judith, too, was dissolving as far as my senses were concerned. I don't know why it was that her magnificent body, exuberant and sensual, had ceased to stimulate in me the reproductive instinct, or rather the precursor of that instinct that is erotic desire. All kinds of complications had been awoken in my consciousness to support that refusal. 'I'm getting short of breath,' my mind said every time the sexual impulse drove me to unite myself with Judith. 'If I go on, I'll die,' a voice said in the middle of our embraces. Without the anguish of jealousy, in any case, that extraordinarily beautiful girl was no longer as attractive to me as she had been before. To my aid, in that unbearable situation, came one of those events that often occur in a human life. Misfortune, conflict,

critical events pile up, assuming reality all at once. Suddenly, in
those days of war and farewells, a telegram from Rachel
reached me: 'Your mother dead stop. Take the first train stop.
Your family is close to you in your grief. Stop.'

Yes, the misfortunes had come all at once. That evening I
took the train to go and bury my mother. The money
advanced to me barely covered the ticket. And once again,
during the journey I was persecuted, with renewed violence,
by images of Judith's betrayals. Into my mind swam countless
episodes linked to the memory of my mother, her sweet face
appeared in my imagination in situations both sad and happy,
but those visions were always superimposed with apparitions
of Judith, her affairs, her desires. The harder I tried to rediscover my mother's innocence within myself, the more the
images of Judith distracted me from the goal of my efforts.
Several times I was on the point of getting off the train to go
back and burst into Judith's apartment to surprise her with a
secret lover, and triumphantly tell her to her face that she had
always lied to me. I was etching out in my mind the dramatic
sentences I would utter the moment the irrefutable truth was
revealed, when I thought I saw before me, standing in the
darkness of the compartment, the figure of my mother. 'What
do you want to tell me?' I asked softly, since someone had
once explained to me that it was important to stay calm when
visited by a ghost. My mother smiled at me without saying
anything and then disappeared. I began to shiver.

The pain in my teeth sent a very powerful impulse to my
brain. I thought about myself, my teeth, my mother: for the
first time in ages Judith had vanished from my mind. I
remembered a summer evening when my mother and I were

going to fetch the fresh milk from a peasant in the village where my father had sent us on holiday. The sky was filled with stars, and my mother sang a song. 'Where are you, where have you run to?' I murmured, and a lump came to my throat. I wept with a painful sense of futility, and then I went to sleep. I awoke ten hours later, the moment the train pulled into my city's Eastern Station. I had gone through passport and baggage control half asleep, without noticing what was going on. When the train arrived Rachel, my children and grandchildren were lined up on the pavement. One by one they pressed up against me: they were haggard, they even seemed dirty to me, their eyes were lined with red. They led me to the funeral, which Rachel had organized down to its finest details.

It was not possible for me to see my mother, the coffin was already closed. Had my wife planned that as well, to keep every last fragment of emotion for herself? Rachel never denied or confirmed it. Throughout the brief burial ceremony she looked at me questioningly. 'The only truth is here. Why don't you come back to us, given that everything ends here, in death? Mend your ways.' That was what her expression seemed to be saying to me. All the mistakes, the lies in my life suddenly made themselves felt with the bitterness of repentance. The moment they began to lower the coffin into the hole, a short, hoarse howl erupted from my throat. 'Is it all over?' I asked myself. Leah pressed herself to me. At that moment I saw Judith again. 'She's sure to be in the arms of a lover. That's how she likes to start the day.' The thought prevented me from taking leave of my mother, completely invading my consciousness and coming back to present me, over and over again, with the same images of embrace and orgasm. I awoke from those fantasies only when someone came over and, with a little knife, cut my shirt at the level of my heart. I looked at the grave and said the prayer that I had to recite, but the terrible jealousy wouldn't let me think about what I was doing and the place where I was. I could think only of Judith and the pain of the abscess grew even stronger.

'We'll never leave you,' Rachel said at the end of the ceremony. I didn't know if it was a promise or a threat. I took note of both. My dull pain submerged everything. Everything seemed opaque and confused, apart from the feeling of jealousy, far too sharp and well-defined, that I felt for Judith. Leaving the cemetery on Kozma Street, I climbed aboard a slow and ramshackle tram, asking my wife and children to leave me alone. I wept all the way to People's Theatre Street.

That afternoon I asked Leah to drive me to the surgery of Dr Hönig, who examined UL7 and announced that he would only be able to extract the tooth a few days later: the severe inflammation had to be reduced before anything could be done. I insisted that he remove the tooth immediately. 'I'll bear the extra pain caused by the abscess.'

'But you know the abscess will prevent the action of the anaesthetic? The moment the tooth is extracted you're going to feel a terrible pain.'

'It doesn't matter. I'll take responsibility for that,' I said.

'But I won't!' yelled the dentist. 'I won't take responsibility for hurting you or anyone else. My profession forbids it. Go away and take the tooth out yourself if you won't listen to me.'

'That's exactly what I'm going to do,' I replied. 'And then it will be your responsibility.'

The dentist looked at me in astonishment. 'Are you black-mailing me?' he asked.

'Yes. What'll I do? Shall I go?' My daughter was on tenter-hooks and, rebuking me as though I was a disobedient child, exhorted me to be a man. She couldn't have said anything worse, since the word suddenly conjured up the battle between the sexes and my stormy affair with Judith. 'How dare you talk to your father like that!' I thundered. 'Shame on you! I never want to see you again!' I left the surgery, slamming the door, and found myself back in the heart of the Eighth District.

The May air was mild, girls in light dresses were strolling around Matthias Square. Where was I to go? I was a stranger here, too, in my own homeland. I sat down on a bench, thought for five minutes, and then walked towards the old house on Karpfenstein Street, where I had lived for so many years with Rachel and the children. When I rang the bell my heart was thumping. Rachel opened the door and said unceremoniously, 'Come in.' For a moment I thought of Judith, of my demented love for her. Then I bit the bullet and went in, promising myself once again to stay only as long as I had to if I was to reflect on the immediate future. I had already decided to take the first train and go back to Judith. Where she was concerned my will, my decisions were annulled, useless. But in this respect, too, my wife also proved greatly superior. Rachel calmly asked about the state of UL7 and, having heard how things had gone with our daughter's dentist, she offered to carry out the extraction herself. She wanted to examine UL7, to test how mobile it was. 'How ghastly! It's like a child's milk tooth.' She went and got some thread, tied one end to

UL7 and the other to the door-handle, and began to yank on my unfortunate tooth with all the fury of a hangman. UL7, fixed to my jaw only by its ligaments, refused to yield. Rachel's grotesque enthusiasm didn't seem to subside, equalled in every respect by my pain and passivity: I was probably allowing her to exact her revenge for all my mistakes as a husband. All of a sudden I felt a searing and unimaginable pain. I yelled with all my strength, tore the thread from my mouth and ran away. I couldn't take that infernal torture. I caught the train again, spent another night in the compartment that smelled of dust and grease, and returned to Judith for the last time.

I reached her apartment unannounced. I opened the door with trembling hands. I was sure I would find her in bed with someone. But the apartment was empty. Judith had already gone out, or perhaps she hadn't come home. I waited all day, sitting on a couch, mulling over the questions of my life, and the unbearable suffering it had caused me. Judith came home at eight. I looked at her, silently, and greeted her with a kiss on the cheek. I was amazed to find that she was a complete stranger to me. In some recess of my soul (represented on earth by LL1) I had finished with her. Whether she betrayed me or not was a matter of indifference to me. Her betrayals, like our love, had descended into play-acting of a very low kind. When she embraced me and spoke to me, I became aware of an inexplicable unease. Not only had Judith become a stranger to me, she actually annoyed me. How could that be? What were these human feelings that were born and vanished from one moment to the next? Judith, who had until two days before seemed the alpha and omega of my universe, now barely existed in my senses and my thoughts.

'Are you ill?' she asked tenderly. 'What can I do for you, my love? My love!' She kissed me on the forehead, on the eyes, at once maternal and childish. It still left me indifferent. 'I'll comfort you, I'll be your mother and your lover.' It was all to no avail, this play-acting struck me not only as silly and deranged, but as dishonest. I went to bed beside her and immediately fell asleep. The abscess had subsided and UL7 let me rest. I slept until ten.

The next day I got up and went to see Dr Fischer, to ask him to clean LL1 and extract UL7 without delay. Fischer listened to me and did as I requested. I left his surgery with a sense of freedom that I had never felt before. At my feet I saw the city, the Great Whore sitting on the waters. I presented myself at the hotel and returned to my job for a few days, and once I had earned enough money to return to my homeland, I got on the train without saying goodbye to Judith who had, in any case, only come to see me once during that time. She was very intelligent and sensitive. She had understood that there were no longer any bonds of any kind between us. She was resigned. She had come to bring me a little parcel, containing two pairs of socks and a shirt: all my belongings. Seeing her arrive, I had locked myself in the concierge's lumber-room, waiting for her to go away.

Some months later, in the city of my birth, after UL7, UL8 was extracted as well, and my cheek, no longer having the support of those teeth, caved in. Suddenly I was old. And as an old man I gave myself back to Rachel, my wretched, tender jailer. Of Judith, the woman I had loved more than any other in my life, I had only vague memories: my brain, over the age of fifty, had lost too many cells to form a real memory of her. LL1 stopped blackening: it stayed white and solid until it too left me, the last of the thirty-two intruders in my black oral cavity. When Dr Metzger extracted it, I felt a sense of relief: the final, vague smell of erotic obsession had left me. Now I could confront the 'other' with all the compassion it needed. Every day, I started giving a small share of my pathetic pension to a beggar of the community where my father had, for a time, been the ritual butcher. The great upheavals of these last fifteen years have left me indifferent, I have ceased to be 'in business', lest I bring into the world some form of business that would be rather difficult to manage, full of unpredictable dangers: all the more since we know so little, perhaps nothing, of our opposite number.

DENTURES

Since I became edentulous (I don't count the four tooth-pillars left me as abutments to support my dentures), I have understood once and for all that my aspiration was always to attain a state like that of the newborn. It's true, without my prosthesis I can't tear bits of meat to pieces with my incisors to grind them with my molars and swallow them as pulp. I can't bite into apples – what a symbolic fruit! – or shatter nuts or other similar natural products.

I can chew soft bread, boiled potatoes, vegetables, soft fruit like melon, citrus fruits, ripe pears.

My whole life has changed. The tooth, that white stranger, is no longer fixed within me to torture me. If I want to, I can take my teeth out, put them in a glass of water, take them out again and put them back in my mouth.

'You're always fiddling with your false teeth, touching them, adjusting them, you're revolting!' Rachel often scolds me.

'I know,' I answer. 'But when we got married you must have known there was a toothless and disgusting old man hiding inside me. It was just a matter of a few decades.'

'When you get married you don't think of things like that,' she went on.

'Dreadful. You should have to take two courses before you get married: one in child-rearing and another in the use of dentures.'

To tell the truth, in this winter of my life, Rachel has always been by my side, steadfast in her fidelity. She went with me to all the clinics, to all the laboratories. Dr Metzger knew two of them: I went to the one that was better equipped, which was looked after by deaf-mute technicians. A tousle-haired young man, the only one who could speak, albeit very slowly and with alarming linguistic distortions, handed me a catalogue and began to describe its contents.

'You see, these are the fundamental types. You'll find the prices on the final pages. The three main types are: fixed-movable, removable and fixed. The application procedures are described here.'

I opted for the type called 'removable'.

'There are various kinds of anchorage,' the young man went on with his explanation, 'the Dolder bar model, the Dalla Bona sphere type, the Gerber precision attachment, and many others. With you I'm going to use the Dolder bar.'

He showed me three drawings and a number of photographs for the various types of attachment. 'You'll come out looking like a young man, you'll see.'

A mould was made of the ridges of my gums and my remaining teeth, including UR7, LR7 and LL2. I consider these my mouth's 'unknown soldiers'. There is no story connected to their tempestuous existence, apart from fleeting caries and equally fleeting treatments. They belong to the formless mass of suffering of which the world is made. I had to bite various kinds of paste made of seaweed. Over the weeks that followed, the slaughter began. One after another, two per session, eight teeth were extracted from me. Tears came to my eyes as I thought how my body, my very self, was being taken to pieces. At night I dreamed of those extractions, as if I was being decapitated.

Dr Metzger, a man with a broad face and thick, grey pomaded hair, comforted me as executioners do. 'It'll just take a moment, you'll see.'

But for me those weeks were like an eternity of pain and struggle. I asked to see every tooth that had been extracted, and as I contemplated it for a few seconds, episodes from my life came to mind, faces of people I had loved. Sometimes I burst into tears and I couldn't even bite my lips to hold them back. That struggle passed as well, and the transformation voided me of all human feelings. I didn't want to see anyone, neither my children, nor my few friends, nor the inhabitants of the district. In any case, my face was completely different, unrecognizable even to myself. There were no longer any teeth to support my cheeks and lips: I too had become a Leonardo caricature.

When the last tooth had been taken out, they made my occlusal registration, put the mould in a metal box called a 'mitten' and effected the definitive moulding of the denture. Then it was given straight to Dr Metzger, and from him to me.

'Open your mouth and don't make a fuss,' the dentist said the first time I tested the final denture.

'I feel as if I'm in the hands of an executioner and we're making our way towards the gallows,' I moaned. Metzger roared with laughter.

'He's got a pretty macabre imagination, your husband,' he said to Rachel.

'He doesn't mean it,' she answered complacently. Dr Metzger laughed again, and then put the dentures in my mouth. I felt as if the corpse of a whale had entered my oral cavity. This sensation lasted a few minutes, and then my mind got used to its presence. Now I had my teeth back, as fake as we are ourselves, our expression, our movements. There I stood, motionless, with that vast foreign body biting and biting again with my toothless gums. I started to vomit and ran to the bathroom. When I came back Dr Metzger showed me a magazine illustrating the possible illnesses that accompany the use of dentures.

'The most frequent is caused by fungi like candida albicans, then there's Stevens-Johnson syndrome, fatal in certain cases, Crohn's disease, Addison's anaemia, Hunzicker-Laugier's disease, multiform erythema of unknown origin, which causes large red stains on the oral mucosa, and which unfortunately, in its turn, can be as fatal as the life-threatening pemphygus. Then there's Hodgkin's syndrome, Ritter's disease, Peutz-Jeghers' syndrome and many more besides. Xerostomia, for example, the reduction of salival flow, is very unpleasant. But you're still young, and the final stage, when you no longer care about anything, when you throw your dentures on the floor and put them back in your mouth the next day, that time's a long way off.'

'Don't scare my husband, doctor, I beg you. He frightens easily. His whole life has been lived under the shadow of fear.'

'Fear!' Dr Metzger exclaimed. 'Fear's not so contemptible. It's the driving force behind many great deeds. Some people despise it in the name of that popular thing called stress. But fear, which flattens us like cockroaches in the darkness, which makes us contract like worms, quiver like dogs, fear is life. Anguish is nothing but a miserable lie.'

'Let's forget those miserable things, please. Tell him what he'll be able to eat,' Rachel intervened, her philosophy encompassing nutrition. What a great nurse she had been!

'You'll be able to eat anything!' Metzger hurried to assure me. 'But I must say this to you, my dear lady. Dentures, unfortunately, almost always end up in the garbage. The minute you die, some sweet soul always decides to throw them there, among the rags, gauzes, syringes, rotting peel, leftovers, dust. All that delicate work for nothing.'

'Why does he want to torment me like this?' I wondered. 'Who's he taking revenge on? Maybe everyone wants to be avenged for being born.'

I took my Rachel by the arm and we left Dr Metzger's surgery to walk back to Karpfenstein Street. The usual hobbling old ladies, the usual drunks populated the dark streets of the district. They were probably the final witnesses to a form of life already in the process of extinction.

In those streets and in that sunset I thought about the products of the new biological sciences: creatures with two heads, ten hands, capable of synthesizing chlorophyll with their own vertebrate bodies and similar prodigies. I thought I felt my gums filled with teeth newly grown thanks to a hormone that reactivated the gene of dentition. I closed my eyes and stood still. I haven't the breath to exert myself for any length of time. Rachel smiled at me and gave me two or three taps of encouragement on the arm.

We started walking again like that, taking little pauses, while on every continent, in various countries, people were running, impelled by revolutions, wars, massacres, and spectral images arose in houses, in deserts, in ships lost on remote oceans. The Day of Judgement had already been sealed in the circuits of an electronic calculator primed to set off intelligent machines, flying across steppe or tundra, over herds of terrified animals, that would send signals to rockets filled with awesome amounts of destructive energy which, emerging from subterranean depots, would begin their flight towards every corner of the earth to confirm, with their spectacular explosion, the School of Babylon's verdict on the question of whether the creation of man had been a good or an evil thing. Just as Dr Metzger had said: all that delicate work for nothing.